I0618934

Nothing to Lose

The Pocket Watch Chronicles

By

Ceci Giltenan

This is a work of fiction. The characters, incidents, locations and
dialogues in this book are of the author's imagination and are not to be

construed as real. Any resemblance to actual events or persons, living or dead, is completely coincidental. Any actual locations mentioned in this book are used fictitiously.

No part of this book may be reproduced or transmitted in any form or by any means, electronic or mechanical, including photocopying, recording, or by any information storage and retrieval system, without permission in writing from the author.

All rights are retained by the author. No part of this book may be reproduced or transmitted in any form or by any means, electronic or mechanical, including photocopying, recording, or by any information storage and retrieval system, without permission in writing from the publisher except in the case of brief quotations embodied in critical articles or reviews. The unauthorized reproduction, sharing, or distribution of this copyrighted work is illegal. Criminal copyright infringement, including infringement without monetary gain, is investigated by the FBI and is punishable by up to five years in federal prison and a fine of $250,000.

Copyright 2017 by Ceci Giltenan
www.duncurra.com

Cover Design: Earthly Charms

ISBN-10: 1-942623-67-4
ISBN-13: 978-1-942623-67-0
Produced in the USA

Dedication

To Lily Baldwin, without whom I would still be staring at the screen trying to write this book. Thank you for helping awaken my muse again and pulling me out of the block I found myself in. You are one of the very bright lights in my life and I adore you.

And, to my soulmate, my beloved husband, Eamon.

Acknowledgements

Thank you to my friend, Author H.D. Smith for the late night chat about possibilities that gave birth to *The Choice*, in which *Nothing to Lose* was originally published.

Also, thank you to Andrew Lawston, the translator of Giacomo Casanova's book: *The Story of my Escape from the Prisons of the Republic of Venice, otherwise known as 'The Leads.'* The book was a surprisingly fun read and was the source material for a section of *Nothing to Lose*.

"One's philosophy is not best expressed in words; it is expressed in the choices one makes…and the choices we make are ultimately our responsibility."

~ Eleanor Roosevelt

Prologue

The place you find yourself
Now

Gertrude walked into the room and smiled. "Hello. Do ye mind if I come in?"

No response.

"Ye there…yes ye, reading this book. Do ye mind if I come in?" Gertrude smiled at the reader's perplexed expression. "Surprised I'm here for a chat, are ye? Ye mean a character in a book has never spoken to ye before? Well, I guess I can understand that. It's a bit like breaking the fourth wall, isn't it—like a television character speaking directly to ye from the screen? It simply isn't done." Gertrude chuckled. Clearly, the fact that something *simply isn't done*, didn't bother her in the least.

"Or maybe we've had this chat before. My memory can be a bit spotty at times. In any event, I do apologize if ye're finding this a bit awkward, but I really do need to speak with ye, and I promise I won't stay long. Just keep right on reading. Frankly, if ye ever want me to leave, ye'll have to keep reading to get past this bit."

Nothing to Lose

The old woman glanced about, taking in her surroundings. "Lovely place ye've got here." She chuckled again. "No, pet, I'm not talking about the space around ye—I can't see that. This brain and consciousness of yers is absolutely remarkable. It allows ye to open a book and be transported into it. It affords ye limitless possibilities. 'Tis yer mind that gives me life and form. Yer imagination very literally wills me into existence. So while, ye're at it, ye wouldn't mind shaving a few pounds off me would ye? Think of me as a stately—but svelt—elegant, mature woman of indeterminate age. That's it, pet. Now, if ye don't mind, could ye imagine a full-length mirror, so I can see myself?"

Without warning, at the mere mention of the word mirror, one appeared. "That's the ticket." She perused her reflection. "Well, it isn't *exactly* what I had in mind, but then 'tis what suits yer sensibilities, so I'll take it."

She glanced over her shoulder. "Upon my word, where did that pink elephant come from? There, ye saw it too, didn't ye?" Gertrude laughed. "Oh, pet, I was just having one over on ye. 'Tis the oldest trick in the book. Ye can't *not* think of something, once the suggestion is made. So, do be a dear and think me up a nice place to sit while we chat."

And just as the pink elephant had, a chair appeared. "Come now, something a bit more comfy than that would be nice. Perhaps a rocking chair. Yes, there we are. Perfect. I do love a good rocking chair."

Gertrude sat down, making herself comfortable. "Now, as I said, I won't stay long, but there are a few things I need to make clear before ye settle down into the story. If ye've read any of the other Pocket Watch Chronicles, ye might recognize me, but even so ye probably don't know *exactly* who I am. And if this is the first of the Chronicles ye've read, no worries. Ye're on equal footing with everyone else. So don't put the book down and go running to find another one. It absolutely isn't necessary. This book completely stands alone."

She frowned for a moment. "Where was I? Oh, yes, I remember now, I am about to tell ye who I am." She sat up a little straighter. "I am an immortal spirit. I have existed since the dawn of time, from the first moment of creation. Throughout history we have been given different names. Among them are: angel, fairy, muse, spirit guide, messenger, eudaemon, dakini, Deva, elemental spirit, Gandharva, watchers, Grigori, one of the ancients, or a servant of the Divine. Sadly though, all human language is painfully imprecise and human understanding limited. There is no one word that sums up our true nature. So choose the name that works best for ye."

She smiled. "It's perfectly fine if you don't believe in any of these things. We can accomplish what has to be done whether ye believe or not. Our purpose is to guide humans, helping them to discern the Creator's will. We are each given unique skills and tools to aid us and we have but three rules. We cannot lie. We cannot break a promise. And, above all else, we cannot interfere with a human's free will."

Gertrude steepled her fingers under her chin for a moment. "This last point is often the hardest to understand. What if the person we are trying to guide doesn't listen, or says *no* or intentionally tries to circumvent the Creator's will? Well, very simply put, when humans close doors, we open windows. There is usually more than one way to accomplish anything.

"In this story, *Nothing to Lose*, the heroine, Sara, will be given a choice whether or not to travel back in time. Deciding that she has…well…*nothing to lose*, she takes the chance and travels to eighteenth century Venice. It is the adventure of a lifetime for a romance author."

Gertrude smiled broadly. "Now you might be wondering what would have happened if she had made the other choice. As I said, sometimes we have to open windows.

You can find out how by reading *What if I Fall*. It is a completely different story that explores the results of a different choice. The two books are related but can be read in either order. Hmm, perhaps that's where I've seen ye before."

The elderly woman, rose gracefully from the rocking chair. "Well now, I've taken up enough of yer time, so I'd best be going. If ye decide to read *Nothing to Lose* when ye're done with this one, I'll be seeing ye again."

And in the blink of an eye, she was gone.

Chapter 1

Sara Wells had been looking forward to this vacation for months. She had never visited Venice. Everyone said it was one of the most beautiful, romantic cities in Europe. A romance author really should visit the most romantic city in Europe, shouldn't she? But every time she'd suggested it to Mark, her boyfriend, he found reasons not to go. And each time he explained those reasons, they seemed perfectly logical.

So they went river rafting in Pennsylvania and West Virginia, gambling in Vegas and Atlantic City, and skiing in Aspen and Tahoe. The fact that she didn't enjoy rafting and didn't know how to gamble or ski didn't really matter; she loved being with him. He always seemed to work his charm and she became excited about anything they did together. And everything they did was done in style.

Mark's family had made millions with Holland Imports, a series of automobile dealerships that sold pre-owned luxury cars. Mark was a brilliant salesman and already a millionaire in his own right.

It came as a total shock when he suggested they fly to Venice, spend a few days there and then board a ship for a fourteen-day cruise of the Greek islands. Finally, they were going to do something she had longed to do, and it had been his idea. She'd been so excited she packed three days early and could scarcely sleep the night before they left. She didn't even mind the fact that Mark's best friend, Benjamin Talbot, and his newest girlfriend, Daphne Cheswick, were going with them. She didn't care who was with them; it was Venice and the Greek Islands.

Now, she sat alone, sipping coffee at a café on the Grand Canal, within sight of the Rialto Bridge. If that wasn't bad enough, this was the second day she'd wandered the streets of romantic Venice on her own.

When they'd arrived yesterday, Mark had begged off. "Sara, honey, the jetlag has wiped me out. Give me a day to rest and then I'll be a hundred percent yours. I think Benjamin is going to the casino. Maybe you can tag along with them."

"I'm not going to *tag along* with Benjamin and his Barbie doll."

"Suit yourself. But it's a shame for you to miss the sights of Venice just because I'm a light-weight traveler."

"I have no intention of missing Venice. I just wish you'd come with me. You'll get over jetlag faster if you just stay up."

"Sweetheart, if it means so much to you I'll go with you. I fear I'll be a terrible wet blanket though. I really am exhausted. I can't sleep on a plane like you can."

"It was business class, Mark. You could lay completely flat and you still didn't sleep?"

"Not a wink. I was too enthralled watching my beautiful girl sleep to close my own eyes."

She laughed. "Stop. You did not watch me sleep all night."

He grinned at her. "How do you know? You were asleep."

"I suppose I was."

"And that is why you are fresh as a daisy and ready to explore, while I'm beat. But if you really want me to…"

"No, it's okay. I'll tool around on my own for a while."

"That's why I love you, sweetie." He kissed her. "While you're out *tooling around*, see if you can find a good restaurant and we'll go out for a nice dinner. Maybe sushi or Chinese."

"In Venice? Are you kidding?"

Mark laughed. "Yes. I'm kidding." He kissed her again. "I'll see you later. Give me about four hours."

She had found a lovely restaurant in her wanderings. Thankfully, Benjamin and Daphne had plans of their own, so she and Mark had dinner alone. It was wonderful. Afterward they took a spectacular gondola ride, then wound their way through the streets of Venice, hand in hand. It was truly the most romantic place she had ever visited.

When they finally returned to the hotel, Mark gave her a toe-curling kiss in the elevator. "I've always wanted to do that."

Sara blushed. "Mark, there's a security camera."

He shrugged. "So what. We are in love and in Italy. No one cares if we kiss in the middle of San Marco square."

Thankfully the elevator reached their floor before Mark got any other ideas.

When they entered their room, Sara gave him a quick kiss. "I'll be right back."

"Don't keep me waiting long, beautiful. I don't think I can stand it."

Sara giggled as she ducked into the bathroom. She brushed her teeth, had a quick wash to rid herself of the grime of the day and slipped into the filmy silk nightgown she had bought for the trip. It had only taken her a couple minutes, but when she slid into bed beside Mark, he was asleep.

She shook him a little, hoping he was just dozing lightly, but he mumbled something unintelligible, rolled over, and started snoring.

Sara sighed. After his day sleeping, it surprised her that he had fallen asleep so quickly, but she figured it was better to start the cruise well-rested.

She'd crawled out of bed and changed into another nightgown, planning to save the new one for an occasion when he was awake enough to appreciate it.

This morning, when they'd awakened, Mark complained of a headache. "I'm sorry, beautiful, it must have been the red wine last night."

"Red wine doesn't usually give you a headache."

"No, but I don't usually drink it exhausted and dehydrated. I think it went to my head. There is no other explanation for why I fell asleep on my beautiful, sexy girlfriend. I'm sorry, babe. I'm afraid walking around in this heat will only make things worse."

"It's okay. It's just a shame that you won't get to see much of Venice."

"When I'm with you, I don't see anything else anyway." He slid his hand behind her neck and kissed her deeply, leaving her breathless and wanting more when he pulled away. "I love you, babe. Let me get a little more rest and try to get rid of this headache and I promise I'll make it up to you tonight."

"All right. Take some aspirin and rest. I'll just sit at the desk and work on my book."

"You are the best." He gave her another quick kiss. "But I'll feel terrible if you miss out because of my headache. Go on. Do some more exploring. If the headache goes away soon, I'll call your cell and we can meet somewhere."

"Okay. If I don't hear from you, I'll be back by noon so we can check out."

"There's no need to cut your day that short. I requested a late check-out. We just have to board the ship before four-thirty. I figure we'll have plenty of time if we leave here around three."

"Okay. I can't imagine that your headache won't be gone before then. Maybe we can meet for lunch?"

"Sounds great. I'm sure I'll feel up to it by then. I'll call you."

That had been hours ago and he hadn't called. She tried to call him a couple of times, but it went straight to voicemail. He must have turned his phone off. She'd finally given up and ate lunch alone. It was almost two now; they'd planned to leave for the ship at three. As soon as she finished her coffee, she'd walk back to their hotel.

Just then, a well-dressed, older woman stopped beside her. "Pardon me, dear, would ye mind if I joined ye? All the tables are full and I'm in desperate need of a cup of tea." She had a light Scottish accent and a warm smile.

"No, not at all. I was just leaving anyway."

"Now, lass, don't rush off on my account. I wouldn't mind a bit of company and a wee chat while I have my tea."

"I suppose I have a few minutes."

"Excellent." She held out her hand. "My name's Gertrude."

Sara shook her hand. "It's nice to meet you, Gertrude. I'm Sara."

Gertrude gave a little nod of her head. "The pleasure's mine." She motioned to the waiter and ordered a cup of tea in perfect Italian. "Will ye have another cup of coffee? Is that a latte?"

"Yes, thank you."

Gertrude ordered the coffee and sat in the chair across from Sara. "Now, lass, tell me a bit about yourself."

"There's not much to tell. My name is Sara Wells, I live in Maryland, just outside of Washington, and I'm an author."

"An author? My, how interesting. What sorts of books do ye write?"

Sara smiled. The answer to that question usually elicited one of two responses. People's faces either lit up and they asked about her books, or they smiled politely, saying something like, "I don't really read *romance*." She was willing to bet Gertrude would be in the latter group.

"I write romance."

Gertrude's response surprised her. "Do ye? My, how fascinating. What subgenre do ye prefer?" She appeared truly interested.

"I love fantasy. I have written both contemporary and historical shifter novels. But I have also written regular historical romance."

"And do ye write under yer own name?"

"No, my name sounds dull. Sara Wells writes owners' manuals or standard operating procedures. I use the pseudonym Arieta DeCosta."

"Well, I don't think Sara Wells sounds dull, but I can see the appeal of *Arieta DeCosta*." She pronounced the pseudonym with a light Italian accent. "Tell me, *Arieta*, why are ye in such a beautiful, romantic city alone?"

"I'm not alone. I'm here with my boyfriend."

Gertrude glanced around. "Oh, I'm sorry to intrude. I only saw one cup and assumed ye were alone. Has he gone to the loo?"

"You aren't intruding. He isn't with me at this café, but he is here in Venice."

"What on earth is he thinking, going off by himself and leaving such a beautiful lass alone?"

Sara laughed. "Thank you for the compliment but he didn't exactly go off on his own. He woke this morning with a bad headache and stayed in the hotel to rest a little."

"I see. Well I hope he's feeling better soon."

"Thanks. So do I."

The waiter arrived with Gertrude's tea and another latte for Sara. The elderly woman stirred a little milk and sugar in her tea, took a sip and gave a satisfied sigh before turning her attention back to Sara. "So, ye write romance and ye enjoy fantasy. Have ye ever considered time-travel?"

"Oh, I love the idea of it. But I haven't worked out a really good way to do it, and then too, all the rules make it a challenge."

"What rules?"

"Oh, you know. You can't change anything without risking changing the future. *The Butterfly Effect*."

"The butterfly effect?"

Sara nodded. "A couple of years ago there was a time-travel movie with that title. But the butterfly effect is the part of chaos theory that suggests even something as small as stepping on a butterfly in the past could have huge consequences for the future."

"Oh that's a lot of rot. I believe the universe unfolds as it should in spite of what humans do."

Sara smiled. "Perhaps, but then there is the issue of returning to the present."

"Why is that an issue?"

"Well, my novels are romances. The hero and heroine must have their happily ever after together. Therefore, the reader knows at the outset that the time traveler will stay."

"No one ever returns?"

"Not usually. Still, I guess the fact that the time traveler always stays is the least of the hurdles. In all romance, it's a foregone conclusion that the hero and heroine will be together in the end."

"That's true. Of course, romance is different from real life."

Sara laughed. "Yes, but that's precisely why people read it. They enjoy the fairytale. Reading allows someone to enter a fantasy world where shape shifters, mermaids and a host of other mythical beings dwell. They can leave reality behind for a few hours and travel through space and time. Books bring magic to what is sometimes a mundane world."

"Aye, books certainly can broaden one's imagination. 'Tis a special gift to be able to shake the bonds of reality and soar into the fantastical."

Sara smiled. "I think so, at least."

Gertrude nodded. "So, would ye do it if ye could?"

"Do what?"

"Shake the bonds of reality and travel through time."

"Yes. I love reading."

"Nay, lass, ye misunderstand me. What if ye really had the opportunity to travel through time, would ye take it?"

Sara thought for a moment. "I suppose I might, but it isn't possible."

"What if I told ye it *is* possible?"

"But it isn't."

"Oh, but it *is*."

Sara laughed. "You're not serious. People can't travel through time."

The old woman canted her head. "Tell me, do ye know everything there is to know in this world?"

"No, of course not. No one does."

"Then how can ye be so very certain time travel isn't possible?"

"Because it defies the laws of nature."

"Perhaps, but it doesn't defy the laws of magic."

"There's no such thing as magic."

"Now, lass, ye just finished describing the magic ye yerself create with the written word."

Sara shook her head. The old woman had seemed perfectly normal when she sat down. "That isn't real magic."

"Ye're wrong, it is *very* real magic and so is time travel. If ye put aside yer disbelief for a moment, I'll explain."

The lady might be crazy, but Sara had to hear this. "Okay, tell me about time travel."

"Magic happens in many ways. Ye use written words to bring it into the world. I use other tools." Gertrude reached into her somewhat dated handbag and pulled out a pocket watch on a long chain. "This is my conduit for time-travel."

Sara laughed. "You're funny. A watch...we travel forward in time with each second...it's a great pun."

Gertrude laughed merrily and somehow, just the sound of it lifted Sara's spirits.

"It does seem a bit prosaic doesn't it? But I wasn't making a pun, and it isn't an ordinary pocket watch. Let me show ye." She opened the cover, showing Sara the pocket watch's face.

Sara frowned. "It only has one hand, and it's stopped."

"Aye, because no one is traveling with it at the moment. When it takes ye back in time, this hand will move forward one second for every day you are in the past."

"How does it transport someone to the past?"

"The specifics are beyond even my ability to understand. But very simply, it allows ye to exchange souls with someone else."

"Exchange souls?"

"Aye. Yer soul and consciousness enter someone else's body, in another time."

"And their soul enters my body?"

"Aye, but strictly speaking it isn't usually an even exchange. Ye see, for every day ye're in the past, only a second passes here. Ye'll occupy that person's body for up to sixty days, but when ye return no more than sixty seconds will have passed."

"So the person whose body I enter returns sixty days later with no memory of what happened?"

"Not exactly. Ye see, generally that person will have set events in motion which will ultimately result in their death. Ye'll do something to stop that as soon as ye arrive. But their life was already over, because of some choice they made. If ye return to yer own body, the other person's body will die and their soul will move on."

"If?"

"Aye. Ye must choose to return within the sixty days or ye'll stay forever."

"What happens to the other soul then?"

"Yer body will die and the soul will move on."

"So what about the whole language problem and the risk of drastically changing the future?"

"As I said to ye, there is no risk of ye irreparably changing the future—the universe unfolds as it should. And as to the language problem, it isn't one. A problem that is. While yer soul and memories go with ye, ye'll be in her body, with her brain and memories. Ye'll experience some of her memories immediately, and because language is such an ingrained memory, ye'll know and understand whatever languages she speaks. It will feel as if ye're speaking English. It is also possible that other memories will emerge with time."

"But they might not? How do I explain not remembering anything?"

"Sara, pet, ye're an author. What is the most obvious plot device?"

"Amnesia, I suppose."

"Aye, that's usually the most straightforward, but sometimes it isn't necessary. Each situation is different and how ye handle it is up to ye."

Sara could scarcely believe that she was entertaining this idea, but it was novel and she wanted to know more. "So how does one activate the pocket watch?"

"It is rather simple really. If ye decide to accept it, ye must select a return word. If ye say that word anytime during the sixty days, it will bring ye back to yer own body in your own time, mere seconds after ye left. So ye'll want to pick something ye're unlikely to say accidentally. Then ye say the word and put the pocket watch 'round yer neck, or even in yer pocket before ye go to sleep, and ye'll wake up somewhere else. The pocket watch will be with ye."

"And to come back, I just say the return word."

"Aye. It's as simple as that."

"What if I lose the pocket watch?"

Gertrude chuckled. "Ye can't lose it. The pocket watch manages to be where it's needed. As long as it's in the same time as ye, the return word will work regardless of where it is."

Sara shook her head in amazement, half wishing she had thought this up herself. "So let me make sure I understand. If I accept the pocket watch, before I go to bed I tell it a word and I'll wake up in someone else's body in another time where I'll do something to temporarily prevent that person's death. The hand advances one second for every day I'm in the past. To return home, I must say the word before my sixty days are up. When I return, the person in the past dies. If I don't return, my body here dies."

"Aye. Very concisely stated."

"It's a bit grim."

"I suppose ye could look at it that way, but we all make choices, all of our choices have consequences, and some consequences are more serious than others."

Sara couldn't argue with that. While she was in college, her whole family—her father, mother and younger brother—were killed in a high-speed motor vehicle accident caused by someone who was texting while driving.

Gertrude patted Sara's hand. "You've suffered such consequences."

It hadn't been a question, but Sara nodded, her eyes filling with tears. "Yes, I have."

"I'm sorry. There are no words to express how difficult it is to lose loved ones due to the actions of others."

Sara remained silent for a moment, trying to regain control. She didn't believe the pain of loss would ever dim. When she trusted herself to speak without a quaver in her voice, she said, "Thank you for telling me about the watch. It was a fascinating story."

"So now you have a choice to make."

"A choice?"

"Aye, lass, a choice. Do you want to take the watch and try it, or not?"

"You're serious?"

"Of course I'm serious."

Sara looked at her, flabbergasted. "You expect me to believe the pocket watch actually causes souls to change places?"

"I wouldn't have told ye about it if I didn't expect you to believe it."

Sara was ready to laugh the whole thing off, but something in the old woman's demeanor stopped her. What's more, Sara was filled with absolute assurance that Gertrude's pocket watch could do what she said it could.

"Ye believe me now?"

Sara nodded. "I'm not sure why—maybe you did some sort of Jedi mind control thing—but yes, I believe you."

Gertrude laughed, the enchanting sound again filling Sara with the confidence that all was right with the world.

"I think perhaps you are the first person to ever make that observation. But outside of the cinema, there is no such thing as a Jedi, pet. So, what will it be? Will ye choose to accept the pocket watch or not?"

"I...I..."

Sara was at a loss for words. Could she really do it? Could she really accept the watch and exchange souls with someone? "I...I...how can I? Mark and I leave for a cruise of the Greek islands this afternoon."

"Sara, it will work wherever you are. As long as ye say yer return word within the sixty days, ye'll awake tomorrow morning at sea, with yer whole cruise ahead of ye."

How could she not try this? If it didn't work, she would lose nothing. But if it did work, the rich material she'd have for her historical novels was mind-boggling. *I really have nothing to lose. And maybe I'll be able to do something to prevent the accident. Maybe instead of meeting them at Josh's concert, I could pick them all up and go home a different way.*

Gertrude gave her a sad smile. "Sara, dear, the reason ye don't need to worry about changing the future is that ye'll never be in a position to have that kind of effect. I told ye, the universe unfolds as it should. Nothing ye do will change things that have already happened."

"How did you know that's what I was thinking?"

"Everyone who has ever lost a loved one and was offered the watch wants that."

Sara nodded. "I guess they would."

Gertrude held out her hand with the watch in her palm. "Aye or nay, lass?"

Chapter 2

Sara took a deep breath. She had nothing to lose. "I'll do it." Her mind toyed briefly with what might happen if she fell in love with someone in the past—an occupational hazard she guessed—but she quickly set that concern aside. If what she and Mark had was truly love, and she believed it was, nothing would turn her from him.

"This is an incredible opportunity. Just the mere possibility of going back in time is thrilling. I can't imagine that anyone, at least not any author, would turn it down."

"Oh, but they do."

"Well, I'm not sure I completely believe it will work, but I can't see the harm in trying it. The worst thing that will happen is that I wake up with a useless pocket watch."

"I'm glad ye're open-minded, but I assure ye, it isn't useless. Now, give some thought to the word you'll pick. It should be something you won't say accidentally."

Sara thought for a moment before smiling. "Skywalker. I've always loved Star Wars."

"Skywalker it is then. Be sure to say it to the watch right before you go to sleep."

"Okay. Is there anything else I need to know?"

Gertrude pondered that question, tapping a finger to her lips. "I believe ye know how to swim rather well, don't ye?"

Sara laughed. "When I was a senior in high school, I set a school record for the five-hundred-meter freestyle that still hasn't been broken."

"Excellent. And at one time ye worked as a lifeguard?"

Sara gave her a quizzical look. "Yes, but how did you know that?"

Gertrude smiled. "I know a great many things. For example, were you aware that two-thirds of drowning victims are strong swimmers?"

"Actually, yes."

"So why do they drown?"

"They panic. When someone thinks they cannot get their head above water, they lose the ability to think and reason, instinct makes them struggle uncontrollably. Once they reach that point, they can't even grab onto a floatation ring if it is thrown."

"Correct, very good. I'm sure ye were an outstanding lifeguard."

"I'm not sure I understand what that has to do with time travel."

"Don't ye? Never fear, ye will. Now, I must be leaving." She stood to go.

Sara stood too, offering the old woman her hand. "It was lovely to meet you. Will I see you again?"

Gertrude laughed merrily as she shook Sara's hand. "Only time will tell, lass, only time will tell." She turned and walked towards the Rialto Bridge. She stopped for a moment, looked toward the canal and waved. Sara glanced in the direction Gertrude had waved but there was a lot of traffic in the canal at that time of day and she couldn't see anyone waving back. When she glanced back at Gertrude, the mysterious old woman had disappeared into the crowd.

Sarah stared at the watch in her hand. Could it actually work? Sara hoped so. What an adventure sixty days in another time would be. She could hardly wait to go to sleep that night.

The bells from San Marco began ringing, stirring her from her reverie. It was half-past two. She needed to get back. After paying her bill at the café, she crossed the bridge and found the tiny dark alley that led to their hotel. The first time she'd walked through it she was struck by the fact that the alley seemed untouched by time. There was a small shrine to Saint Joseph in a niche about halfway down the passage. All the talk about time travel had her imagination

35

running wild. What if the ancient alley was actually a time portal that would carry her to medieval Venice? "Hey, that could work. That could be my conduit for time travel," she said aloud to the empty alley. She smiled to herself. Maybe the magic of the pocket watch was just to open her mind to other possibilities. Even if she didn't actually go back in time, she'd just figured out a way to let her readers do it.

She stepped into the hot sunshine in the little square at the other end. Soon one of her characters would be met with a very different sight at the other end of this alley. She grinned. She was going to write a time-travel novel. *Thank you, Gertrude, for giving me the idea.*

She practically skipped into the hotel.

The concierge greeted her. "Good afternoon, *Signorina* Wells. Did you enjoy your morning?" His rich Italian accent transformed the polite greeting into something intimate, almost illicit.

Sara smiled, certain a man with an Italian accent could read the phonebook and make it sound sexy. "Yes, very much, thanks. We'll be leaving soon. Can you arrange a water taxi for us?"

"Mr. Holland has already taken care of that."

"Perfect. Thank you."

When she reached their room, Mark was just stepping out of the shower. His hair was wet and tousled and he had a towel wrapped low around his hips.

He turned towards her and flashed his megawatt smile. "There you are, gorgeous. Right on time. Just give me a minute to dress and we can head to the cruise terminal."

"Great." She had already packed her things so she sat on the bed to wait for him.

"Are you excited about the cruise?" he asked.

"Very excited. I'm kind of anxious to get to the ship." What she was really anxious to do was settle in and write down her story ideas. They were flying through her head at lightning speed now, urged on by the prospect of actually experiencing another time.

"Damn, where did I put my shoes?"

She shrugged, lost in thought.

"Yoo-hoo, Sara, do you think you could wake up and help me find them?

"Oh, sorry, sure. They probably slid under the bed. I'll look." She knelt on the floor and lifted the dust ruffle. "Yup, here they are." She passed them to him, but as she started to stand, she noticed something on the floor by the bed. "What's this?"

She picked it up. "Eww, gross. It's someone's condom wrapper."

Mark frowned. "Wow, I'm surprised housekeeping missed that. Oh well, at least it's not a used condom. Give it to me. I'll throw it away, then we have to hit the road...or the canal I should say."

"Okay." She handed it to him, her nose still scrunched in disgust.

Mark tossed it in the trash basket by the desk. "I wish I had felt well enough to see more of Venice. Did you take a lot of pictures?"

"A few. I'll show you later." She picked up one of the suitcases. "Are you ready to go?"

"Yeah, but I'll take that. Just grab your purse and your carryon."

"Are Benjamin and Daphne going with us?"

"No, they left earlier. We'll meet them for dinner. It's just you and me for now."

Yay. She did a mental happy dance. The more it was just the two of them the better.

Moments later, they were downstairs and a porter was leading them towards the alley to the Grand Canal.

"Ooh, wait a minute. I want to get a picture of this," said Sara.

"Of the alley?" asked both Mark and the porter in unison.

Sara laughed. "Yes, the alley. I have an idea for a book."

Mark grinned. "That's my girl."

~ * ~

By five that evening the ship was at sea and they were comfortably installed in their stateroom, a large suite with a private balcony that looked off the back of the ship. Mark had cracked open the bottle of champagne that awaited them and Sara sipped on a glass while she tapped away at her computer, trying to capture all of her ideas about time travel.

"Sara, this isn't exactly what I had in mind when I asked you on a cruise vacation. Let's go to one of the bars or the casino before we meet up with Benjamin and Daphne."

"You can go on if you want, I'll just be a minute."

"Nah, on second thought, it's better to give Benjamin a little time to cool down. He's beyond pissed that they fouled up the reservation and we didn't get the penthouse."

"Okay." When she'd first heard about it, she thought the whole thing had been entirely ridiculous and she didn't want to be dragged into a discussion about it. She continued writing and Mark switched on the television.

About an hour later, the phone rang. Mark answered it, but Sara paid no attention to his conversation.

Mark hung up the phone. "That was Benjamin."

"Has he calmed down yet?"

"Some. He's mellowing."

She arched an eyebrow at him. "Mellowing?"

He laughed. "Yes, mellowing. He's angry but he's still here. He didn't storm away when his money couldn't fix the foul up."

"That's true." A smile flirted at Sara's lips. Benjamin handled all problems by throwing money at them and, given his deep pockets, he was accustomed to getting his own way. Frankly, it would have been amusing to watch his tried-and-true method fail, but it had all happened before she and Mark arrived on the ship. "So, what did he want?"

"To meet for drinks and go to dinner."

"Okay. I'll just be another minute."

One minute became twenty and by the time they met Benjamin and Daphne, Benjamin was in a foul mood. Knowing it was better to just grin and bear it, Sara plastered on a smile and kept her mouth shut. It was especially irksome when Benjamin spent a good hour complaining about the "general incompetence exhibited by the crew and cruise line," but she was able to ignore the rant, letting her mind drift back into ideas for her book. By dessert, she had worked out much of the plot and couldn't wait to finish getting it down.

As they left the restaurant, Sara turned towards the elevator lobby.

"Where are you going, gorgeous?" Mark asked.

Sara frowned. "Up to our room."

"Babe, were you not paying attention? We all agreed to go to the casino for a while."

The casino? Ugh. "You know I'm not really good at gambling. I don't know much about it."

He kissed her temple. "You don't have to know much. All you have to do is look beautiful and bring me luck.

Reluctantly, she agreed, but soon grew bored watching Mark and Benjamin play as if they were spending Monopoly money. She really wanted to get back to her book idea.

By half-past ten she said, "I'm really tired, Mark. Do you mind if I go back to our suite?"

"Oh, babe, I'm sorry. You were up early and probably are tired. I should have remembered that." He kissed her. "You go on to bed."

She wasn't exactly going to bed, but that was as good an excuse as any.

Daphne patted her on the arm. "Bless your heart. You do look exhausted."

Sara ignored the insincere comment. "Okay, then. I'll see you later, Mark."

He gave her his winning smile. "You bet, babe. I'll join you soon. The casino closes at three."

Five and a half hours wasn't her idea of soon, but it didn't matter. She'd have all the time she needed with her book. As she walked away, she heard Daphne say, "Well, you can't really expect someone like *her* to understand the excitement of high stakes gaming."

Sara found some measure of satisfaction when she heard Benjamin's derisive laugh. "*This* isn't high stakes gaming."

When she reached the suite, she pulled on comfortable pajamas and got lost in her writing. She reached a stopping point a little before midnight, tired but very happy with her progress.

She retrieved the pocket watch and climbed into bed. Mark would be gone for hours still. If the watch worked, she'd travel to the past, spend sixty days there and be back well before he even returned from the casino.

"Okay little pocket watch, let's see what you can do. My return word is Skywalker." With that she slipped the chain around her neck and curled up under the covers, falling asleep nearly instantly.

Chapter 3

Sara awoke as her body hit the cool water and she instinctively took a deep breath just before her head went under. *Holy hell, what's happening?* Everything was black. She must have fallen overboard at night, but she wasn't sure how. She tried to kick her way to the surface of the water, but something restricted her legs and it felt as if she were being pulled deeper. It was her clothing. She wore shoes and layer upon layer of clothing.

Layers of clothing? The pocket watch had worked but if she didn't free herself, she was going to drown. First to go were the shoes and stockings. Then she removed a cape like garment from her shoulders. She jerked the long heavy skirts up, freeing her legs so she could kick her way upward. Still weighed down with wet clothing, it took everything in her to reach the surface. The moment her head broke the water, she gasped, filling her lungs with much needed oxygen. She tried to tread water as she worked to remove her clothes but it was nearly impossible to do both. She was going to exhaust herself quickly at this rate so she took a deep breath and allowed herself to sink a little as she searched for openings in her garments.

The heavy outer dress had laces up the front. She found the tie, released it, and managed to loosen the ribbon enough to wriggle out of the dress. This decreased her weight enough that she was able to swim back to the surface and stay there this time. She wore layers of petticoats that untied easily. Within minutes she had shed everything except a silk chemise and the pocket watch that hung around her neck. Completely unburdened now, it took very little energy to tread water, so she took a moment to assess her situation.

The sky was overcast and she was completely enshrouded by the dark of night. The only light came from lanterns on a large galleon not far away. The activity on the deck suggested that something was wrong. Sara assumed the girl in whose body she found herself must have fallen—or jumped—from that ship. It was likely they were working to rescue her. She could just wait, treading water, until they did.

In an effort to figure out where she was, Sara looked around. They were fairly close to land, given the direction the ship was pointing, they must be returning to port. She was certainly within swimming distance. But there was also another ship bearing down on them with full sails. Somehow this distressed her. She felt as if she had to avoid that ship at all costs. Maybe this was one of the other girl's memories pushing through, but in that moment, Sara believed she needed to swim to shore, avoiding both ships.

In fact, she was so certain of this, just in case the white shift she wore might be seen, she swam underwater as long as she could before surfacing for a quick breath and dipping back under again. When she was finally far enough away to be sure the lights from the ship couldn't reach her and reveal her location, her anxiety lessened and she switched to a slow steady freestyle stroke. She tired much sooner than she'd expected to. Just as she'd told Gertrude, she had been a distance swimmer in high school. She still swam almost every day for exercise and should have been able to reach the shore with little difficulty.

But this isn't your body, she reminded herself. She needed to rethink this, or risk tiring and drowning. She flipped over and floated on her back for a while to rest. When she felt able, she turned back over and swam for a while. She repeated this process over and over, until she reached the point that she could barely take five strokes before turning over for a rest. Eventually she did reach land, but she was exhausted.

There was a narrow strip of sand and rocks between the sea and an area of land covered in sea grass. The night was warm and still, only a slight breeze stirred. But soaked and with nothing dry to wrap around her, it was enough to chill her. The tall vegetation would shield her from what little air moved. She crawled across the sand and curled up in the grass, completely spent. She had no idea when or where she was. And while she should probably seek some help, she didn't have the energy to. She laid her head down and gave into sleep.

~ * ~

Benedict MacIan was accustomed to rising before dawn on work days, but he usually tried to sleep a little longer on Sundays. However this morning, the first rays of dawn had barely pinked the sky when something jarred him from sleep. He laid in bed and listened, but nothing broke the early morning stillness of the empty house. He tried to go back to sleep but simply couldn't. Finally, he gave up, rose and dressed.

He went down to his kitchen and made a cup of tea, but even as he sat down to drink it, something nagged at him. He wasn't sure what it was, but decided perhaps a walk on the beach would put this feeling to rest.

Even in this coolest part of the day on the Lido, a narrow island well away from the center of Venice, the morning was warm. It would be a hot day and he was glad he didn't have to go to his shipyard in the Arsenale today.

He walked along the deserted beach, the waters of the Adriatic washing over his feet, wondering what had beckoned to him.

Beckoned? That was an odd choice of words. But now that he thought on it, he knew it was the right word because he felt drawn forward as if someone were calling to him.

Then he saw it. A hundred yards or so down the beach, something had crushed the sea grass and he could glimpse white fabric.

He picked up his pace. When he realized it was a person, he broke into a run. As he drew closer he was able to see more clearly that it was a girl, or a young woman with dark curly hair. She appeared to have crawled across the sand and lay curled up in the grass, wearing nothing but a thin white shift.

When he reached her, he knelt at her side. Her shift was damp and she was cool to the touch. Turning her gently onto her back, he feared the worst. But within seconds, he was able to discern the shallow rise and fall of her chest. He breathed a sigh of relief. She was alive. Maybe only barely, but she was alive. *Thank God.*

He shook her gently. "Miss, miss, can you wake up?" he asked in Venetian.

Eyes fluttered open. It was still too dark to see what color they were. "Where…where…where am I?"

Her words were English. He spoke English but not on a regular basis so he was a bit rusty, but he'd give it a go.

"Miss, you are on the Lido, one of the Venetian islands. What are you doing here?"

She appeared puzzled for a moment. Raising up on one elbow she frowned and looked around. "I'm wet." She rubbed her head and sand from her hand fell onto her face. "And sandy. I, uh…I guess I swam here."

"You swam here? Why on earth would you do that? Did you come from one of the ships?"

Her frown deepened. "I don't know. I don't remember."

"Maybe just start with your name. Can you tell me your name?"

"I'm not sure."

"What do you mean, you're not sure. You can't remember your name?"

"I uh…no. Well, maybe. I think my name is…Sara. Who are you?"

"My name is Benedict MacIan. Where are you from, Sara? Maybe you fell overboard and I simply need to find the right ship."

"I don't know where I'm from. I don't remember."

Benedict frowned at her. "You don't remember who you are and where you're from?"

She furrowed her brow. "No, I don't."

Benedict shook his head. "I'm not sure what's happening, but I think I should get you inside and dry. Can you stand?"

"I...I believe so."

He helped her into a sitting position and then onto her feet, but she swayed, falling forward.

His arms were around her instantly. "Whoa there. Perhaps I should carry you."

He scooped her into his arms. She buried her head against his chest as a trusting child would, and it warmed his heart. He carried her to his home. Even though she was very light, he was tired by the time he arrived.

She'd clearly been through some ordeal. In spite of her memory loss, she didn't have any obvious injuries. Perhaps if she rested, she would recover her memory.

"Sara, I'm going to take you upstairs to a bed. I think after you've slept a while you'll feel better."

"Yes, I think so. I'm utterly exhausted."

He probably should put her in the room that his parents had shared, but there were no linens on the bed. He figured it would be best to let her sleep in his own bed for the moment. He sat her on the edge of the bed. It was the first chance he'd had to take a good look at her. Even sandy, damp, and bedraggled, she was lovely. Small of stature, with dark curly hair, creamy fair skin, and crystal blue eyes. The damp silk shift left nothing to the imagination, revealing the clear outline of gently rounded breasts with pert nipples. She also seemed to have a gold chain around her neck on which hung what might be a locket that nestled between her breasts. He sighed. While he could gaze on this lovely sea nymph for hours, she needed dry clothing and sleep.

"I think it would be better if you slept in a dry garment. If I give you a shirt can you manage to put it on?"

"Yes."

"Good." And yet a very wicked part of him longed to remove that shift himself and explore her beautiful body. He reined in his libido, walked to his wardrobe, and returned with a clean, soft cotton shirt, handing it to her. "I'll turn my back."

"Thank you."

He turned around. The bed creaked slightly as she stood then quickly sat back down.

"Are you all right?"

"Yes. My legs feel like jelly, but I can manage."

Moments later she said, "You can turn back around now."

He did and if he'd thought dressing her in one of his shirts that was many times too large would make her less appealing, he was wrong. He felt the tiniest bit jealous towards that shirt which could caress her silky body with impunity.

"Here, let me help you under the covers." He pulled them back and she lay down, curling onto one side. He settled the bed linens over her. "Are you comfortable?"

"Yes, thank you." She yawned and snuggled into the pillow.

"Then I'll leave you to rest. I'll be downstairs but I'll leave the door to this room ajar. Just call out if you need something."

"Thank you," she whispered, already nearly asleep.

He went back downstairs and headed to the kitchen. He made himself a cup of tea and pondered what to do with the girl. She didn't seem to be injured, just exhausted. By the look of things, she had fallen off of a ship heading into the

Venice lagoon and had managed to swim to the shore of the Lido. Maybe the locket she wore would reveal something about her identity. He'd try to learn a bit more when she awoke.

Chapter 4

When Sara woke next, the bright sun outside and the heat of the room suggested it was well after noon. Hot and confused, she threw the bedclothes back and sat up on the edge of the bed. She'd had a horrible dream about drowning. She ran her hands through her hair only to find a mass of tangled curls with liberal amounts of sand captured in them. *What the hell?* She looked around. This was not her stateroom.

Then she became aware of the weight of a chain around her neck. She felt for the pendant and pulled it out from under the voluminous shirt she wore.

The pocket watch. She had accepted it from Gertrude and had used it. It hadn't been a dream. She had gone to bed on board the ship and awoke in the water, fighting for her life. By some miracle, she'd been able to swim to shore though the body she found herself in was much less fit. Maybe she should just say the word and go home.

But then she remembered being found on the beach by a man. An insanely handsome man. What had he said his name was? He was tall with light golden-brown hair, green eyes, tanned skin that suggested he worked in the sun and a physique the likes of which she had only seen on models in magazines or on the covers of romance novels. And even those had probably been touched up.

Romance novels. It was as if he had stepped straight out of one.

Thoughts of the ancient alley down which she'd walked to get to the hotel yesterday afternoon popped into her head. She'd thought it was a perfect location for a time portal and had already started the story. Now she found herself in the past, still in romantic Venice. She wasn't sure what year it was, but that was a minor, easily solved, detail.

She grinned. This was perfect. Absolutely perfect. The dreamily good-looking man who had carried her from the beach, was about to become the hero in her next novel. If she could get to know him, she could create one of the most well-developed characters ever written and place him in the most realistic setting possible. *Thank you, Gertrude.*

Then she felt a moment of panic. The pocket watch had been in the water, what if it didn't work anymore? She opened it to check for signs of water damage. It seemed to be in perfect condition and she rolled her eyes at herself. *It's a magic pocket watch, goof ball. If it can pull a soul through time, it surely can stand a bit of sea water.*

Taking in her surroundings, she noticed a small pile of clothing had been placed on a chair. Her savior must have found something for her to wear other than his shirt. Perhaps they were his wife's clothes. Sara frowned, not sure why that thought bothered her. She could pattern a hero after him whether he was married in real life or not.

On top of the garments was a tortoise shell comb. *I definitely need that.* A washstand stood in one corner of the room on which sat a bowl and pitcher. Towels hung on the towel bar.

Excellent, she would get cleaned up, dressed, and go exploring.

She stood up and immediately sat back down. Weak and wobbly, her swim had clearly strained the limits of whoever's body she was in. She stood again, this time prepared for the instability. She retrieved the comb and sat back on the edge of the bed. It took ages to untangle the wild mess that was her hair, due in part to the fact that her arms were as feeble as her legs had been. She just couldn't hold them up to her head for very long without having to rest. But eventually she was able to comb out most of the sand, and while impossible to completely control without modern hair products, the dark curls hung down her back temporarily tamed.

Next, she made her way to the washstand. She poured water into the bowl, removed the shirt, and washed the sand and saltwater from her skin. The body she was in was small and very slender, but she wasn't without curves. Her skin was fair and pale as if it had never been exposed to the sun. Which stood to reason, considering the sheer volume of clothing she'd had to fight her way out of to keep from drowning.

Finally, she examined the clothes that had been set out for her. She smiled. Any other woman from her own time might have been a bit confused by all the layers, but Sara had always been fascinated by historical clothing. There had been an old set of World Book Encyclopedias at home when she was growing up. One of the two "C" volumes had a section of yellow pages with colorful images of the clothing people had worn throughout history. Even before she could read, she knew which volume they were in because she could see the section of yellow pages just by looking at the closed book. Once she started writing historical novels, she had done even more research. After all, it was kind of a requirement that characters in romance novels had to undress, and to do that she had to know what they were wearing underneath everything.

Nothing to Lose

She donned the cotton shift first. It had obviously seen quite a bit of use because the cotton was worn and soft.

The next garment, the chemise, resembled a nightgown. It hung loose to the floor but had close fitting, three-quarter length sleeves. As she pulled it over her head, she realized it smelled a bit stale. Not musty, just as if it hadn't been laundered recently. Maybe they weren't his wife's clothes after all.

Then came several petticoats and finally a rust colored cotton gown that laced in the front, conforming to her figure. That was probably a good thing because it might have been too big otherwise. There wasn't a looking glass in the room, but she liked what she saw of the way she looked. She'd always wanted to try on period clothing, but she'd rather imagined herself in a cold climate. These were way too many clothes to wear in this heat. She was glad there hadn't been a corset. She might have spontaneously combusted.

The style of clothing helped her at least figure out what century she'd landed in. Men's clothing styles changed more slowly than women's over time. The clothes the man had been wearing could have been worn in the late seventeenth century all the way through to the early nineteenth century. But the outfit she wore was most likely mid-eighteenth century. She intended to figure it out precisely and there was no time like the present. He'd said he would be downstairs so she'd just go look for him.

She left the room, found the stairs, and holding tightly to the handrail because of her wobbly legs, made her way down. At the bottom of the stairs was a hallway off of which were several doors. Most were ajar, but she wasn't sure she should just go poking her head in them. "Hello," she called softly.

Nothing.

She tried again, a little louder this time. "Hello."

He stepped out of the door at the end of the hall. "Hello. I see you found the clothes I put out for you. They fit you well."

Sara smoothed her hands down the front of her dress. "Yes, thank you." *Oh, hell, just ask.* "Do they belong to your wife?"

He grinned. "Nay, my mother."

"Oh." Sara supposed she would have the opportunity to meet and thank Mrs. Whatever-his-name-is at a later time. "Well, thank you. For everything. I owe you so much and I'm sorry, I know you told me, but I can't quite remember your name."

"That's not surprising. You weren't even sure of *your* name when last we talked. But my name is Benedict MacIan."

She smiled. "I'm pretty sure my name is Sara."

"Aye, that's what you said."

She may as well dive into the amnesiac role with both feet. "And you said we were on one of the Venetian islands—"

"The Lido."

"Right. The Lido. But that's about all I can remember. I don't even know what day it is." Maybe he'd include the year in his answer.

"'Tis Sunday, the ninth day of July. Come to the kitchen and I'll make you a cup of tea."

July ninth, the day I left. How odd. But I still don't know the year. Maybe she could figure it out without just asking. She followed him through the door at the end of the hall.

"Benedict MacIan? That doesn't sound very Ital—I mean Venetian."

He chuckled. "It isn't. I'm a Scotsman. Here, have a seat."

A Scotsman living in Venice? That could make a very good story. She sat at the table as he put a kettle on an iron

60

cook stove, opened the door to the firebox, stoked the fire to bring it to life, and added some coal. Cook stoves only came into use in the latter half of the eighteenth century. This reconfirmed what she had guessed so far about the year.

As he continued to gather what was needed to make tea, she asked, "How long have you lived in Venice? Are you on the Grand Tour?" She knew there was a time when young European men, particularly British gentlemen, spent several years visiting some of the great cities of Europe as part of their education. Venice had been one of the popular destinations.

"Definitely not. I'm not a member of the gentry. I'm just a common Scotsman. My parents were originally from the Isle of Mull, but I've lived here since I was ten years old."

"What brought you to Venice?"

"It's a bit of a winding story. My parents left Mull for Port Glasgow when I was just a wee lad—I think I was about four. They were very poor, but my father was a skilled carpenter. He believed he could make a better life for his family working in the shipyards of Port Glasgow. After a few years, a Venetian merchant, Emilio Santi, took notice of his talent and offered him the opportunity to build ships here. I think initially Da planned to learn what he could, then return to Scotland to find his fortune there. But he fell in love with Venice. Eventually he and Emilio formed a partnership." He laughed. "Santi and MacIan, the soundest vessels on the sea, and like most Venetian ships, works of art in their own right."

"You speak of him in the past tense."

"Aye, neither of my parents are living."

Ah, that would explain why his mother's clothes smelled as if they had been stored for a while. "I'm sorry. What happened?"

"They went back to Scotland for a visit when I was sixteen and got caught up in the rebellion. Da was killed at Culloden and my mother died shortly thereafter. They say she died of a broken heart."

"I'm so very sorry for your loss." Her heart ached for him. She understood only too well what it was like to lose both parents.

"'Twas a long time ago."

"Losing a parent, both parents, is a terrible thing. I—" she stopped herself from saying *lost my parents and brother all at once too*. If she had amnesia, she wouldn't know that. "Uh...that is...I can't imagine that. How long has it been?"

"Over twelve years."

Twelve years. The battle of Culloden was in April 1746. So, Sara had travelled to the year 1758 and her host was twenty-eight years old. This was absolutely amazing. She wanted to know more. This novel was going to be her best yet. "So, you live here alone?"

"Aye."

"And are you a shipbuilder?"

"Aye. I inherited my father's half of the business."

Sara could just imagine him building a ship, shirt off, tight breeches, rippling muscles glistening with sweat. *Oh yeah. You are a spectacular hero. Alberto maybe…no Pietro…no Rafael. Rafael di Santi. Rafe. Son of a shipbuilder.* She needed to see the place he worked. "Is the shipyard nearby? I'd love to see it."

"The shipyard isn't here on the Lido. It's in the Arsenale."

Of course, it is. She'd learned about the history of the Arsenale while sight-seeing yesterday. But that begged the question, "If your business is in the Arsenale, why do you live here? And in such a remote area?"

"As much as my father loved Venice, my mother hated it. She despised the city—there were too many people. She hated the food and the language. She couldn't stand the weather."

"It's beautiful here."

"That was the problem. Of all things, she didn't like the brilliant sunshine. She longed for cold, gray Scotland. She even hated the winters here because while it can get quite cold, there are still lots of sunny days. She said it made her head ache."

"Then she must have really hated this time of year."

"That she did. She simply loathed the summer heat. Stormy Scotland was home and that was where she wanted to be. So, my father built a home for us here on the Lido, well north of the village of Malamoco. It was easy enough for him to cross the lagoon to go to work. He'd hoped the seclusion and proximity to the sea would make her more comfortable."

"It didn't?"

"Only a little. She refused to have anything Venetian-made in her home. She used pewter and crockery rather than the beautiful glassware for which Venice is famous. She wouldn't wear silk or brocade or any of the beautiful fabric made here, preferring wool and linen."

"Wool? Well, no wonder she didn't like the heat."

He nodded and smiled. "Da bought her some beautiful things, even though she generally shunned them. But during the heat of the summer, she did give in and wear some cotton garments like those." He indicated the clothes Sara wore. "But she left them all behind when she and Da went to Scotland. I truly believe her unwillingness to adapt to the smallest thing only made her more homesick."

Sara's romantic heart ached a little for his father. She imagined a man in love with his wife. Wanting only the best for her. Buying her beautiful clothes made of luxurious fabrics which due not only to their expense, but also to sumptuary laws, she couldn't have owned in Scotland. She also imagined his disappointment when she rejected his gifts.

"That's sad. To love someone and want the best for them and yet to be unable to make them happy. It must have been distressing to him."

At that, Benedict stopped what he was doing, giving her a quizzical look. "I've never quite thought of it that way, but I'm sure it was."

She cocked her head to one side. "It must have been upsetting to you, too. It can't have been easy to grow up with a mother who was never happy."

Benedict's brows drew together and he looked as if he were about to say something, but changed his mind. "It was a long time ago. Besides, my history is of little consequence at the moment, whereas yours is paramount. We need to figure out who you are. I thought about it while you were sleeping. The only explanation is that you fell from one of the boats. It shouldn't be too hard to find out. I'll ask around." He poured tea into two cups and placed one in front of her. "Do you take milk and sugar?"

"No, thank you." She said absently. At the mention of finding out who she was, dread had filled her. She remembered the feelings she had experienced moments after she arrived in this body. The feeling that she needed to stay away from the ships at all costs. This could only be one of the other girl's memories pushing through.

"Is something wrong?" He asked.

"No. Well…uh…that is to say…yes I think there is. I can't remember who I am or how I ended up in the water, but I feel like I was trying to escape something. Something dangerous. Do you have to find out where I came from?"

Benedict frowned. "Someone could be worried sick, looking for you. Maybe even believing you are dead. I think it's irresponsible not to find out."

Panic rose in her. "No, please don't. I can't explain why, but I know it would be a mistake."

"Sara, you can't remember anything. How can you be sure of that?"

"Like I said, I don't know. But I'm afraid. I'm not sure how I ended up in the water, but…I fear…I fear…"

What was this fear? It wasn't just for her but for him as well. "I fear it may actually be dangerous—for both of us."

"That isn't likely."

"Nevertheless, I'm certain of it."

"But what am I to do with you?"

"Perhaps you could let me stay here for a little while? Maybe my memories will come back in a few days and I'll know what to do."

~ * ~

Benedict stared at her, not sure what to think. She had appeared completely unconcerned about her profound memory loss, but at simply the suggestion that he try to find out who she was, she was nearly panic-stricken.

"Please, Benedict. I won't be in the way. I promise. Please let me stay with you just for a while."

She seemed so frightened. How could he deny her? "Fine. You can stay for a few days. I'm working on plans for a new ship and I can do that here as easily as I can in the bustle and noise of the shipyard."

She visibly relaxed. "Thank you. I appreciate it immensely."

But her sudden disquiet had set him on edge, too. "Still, if you haven't remembered anything by the end of the week, I'll have to reconsider."

She nodded. "I understand."

Chapter 5

Sara spent the rest of the afternoon and evening chatting with Benedict. She asked questions about his life and his work. At one point, when she feared she was bordering on rudeness, she apologized. "I fear I am being overly inquisitive, but I keep thinking you might say something that jogs my own memory." She suspected it was a lame excuse, but he accepted it and she learned quite a lot about him and a bit about herself.

He had been speaking English to her, because the first words she spoke when he found her were in English. However, the language he spoke daily was Venetian. Additionally, he spoke Scottish Gaelic—the only language his mother would use.

Sara learned that whomever she was, she, too, spoke Venetian but it felt very much like a second language. Still, she figured she should become more accustomed to using it if she wanted to truly experience Venetian culture, so she asked that they communicate as much as possible in Venetian.

If he thought it an odd request, he didn't say so.

Nothing to Lose

When it had been time for bed that night, to her surprise, Benedict showed her to another room.

"This was my parents' room. It hasn't been used in a few years. I aired it out this afternoon and put fresh linens on the bed. You can sleep here for the next few days. There are more of my mother's clothes hanging in the wardrobe. She was very close to your size, perhaps only a bit heavier. Feel free to use whatever you like."

"Thank you, Benedict. Thank you for everything."

"It's my pleasure."

"I'll see you in the morning."

"Yes, but not right away. I'll go to the shipyard at first light as I usually do to get the things I'll need and to let Emilio know I won't be in for the rest of the week. It's likely I'll be back even before you awake, but just in case I'm not, I wanted you to know."

"Thank you. I would have worried."

He smiled. "Then I'll say good night."

"Good night."

Sara had crawled into bed but as tired as her body was, her mind was reeling with the possibilities that lay ahead of her. First things first, she needed to know what her deadline to return home was. Sara had to say the word within sixty day. If today was July ninth, sixty days from now was

September seventh. Still, she wasn't exactly sure how it worked. Was it sixty days to the hour or did she just have to leave sometime on the sixtieth day. She left the twenty-first century just before midnight on July ninth but arrived here in the wee hours of the morning on July ninth. She figured, just to be safe, she should plan to say the word before midnight on September sixth.

That brought her to another concern. How was she going to do this? If she just said the word wherever she was at the time, that's where this body would be found dead. The thought gave her pause. She wouldn't want Benedict to have to deal with her death. In fact, it occurred to her that if she was found dead in his home, he might be accused of murdering her. No, that would not do. Clearly, she had to go somewhere else, but where?

Then it came to her. If those who knew she'd fallen overboard never found her, they would assume she'd drowned. She could put on the shift she'd been wearing and swim out into the Adriatic. When she was far enough out, she could say the word. She would return to her own body and if this body were ever found, it would be consistent with what everyone believed had happened to her.

With those details nailed down, Sara started imagining possible plots worthy of her stalwart hero, Rafe di Santi, and drifted off to sleep.

When she woke the next morning, the sun was barely up. At home, when she wasn't on vacation, she lived by a fairly fixed schedule. She woke early. She didn't set an alarm, it was just what her body was accustomed to. She had breakfast then spent the morning writing. Around eleven, she went out for a while—usually to the gym where she swam or took an exercise class. Then she came home, took a shower, made lunch, and settled down with an iced coffee to write for several more hours. When the time came to stop, she had a glass of wine and made dinner. She enjoyed good food and wine and absolutely loved to cook.

Writing the morning away was out. She couldn't actually do that here. Well, she guessed she could, but it would be a bit pointless because she couldn't take it with her. However, she could play out scenes in her head as she explored this time and place. And she could simply experience what life was like here. Hopefully, she'd remember enough to be able to write the book as soon as she returned. So, she got up, dressed, and made the bed. She looked through Mrs. MacIan's clothes until she found an apron.

When she dressed yesterday, she had remained bare-footed, but it might be good to have a pair of serviceable shoes. She searched the wardrobe, but all she found were two pair of what Sara would have called *slides* or *mules*. Shoes with a low heel that slipped on the foot and didn't have a back or heel strap. One pair was very delicate and beautiful, clearly intended to be worn with a fancy dress. The other pair was a little less dainty. They weren't exactly what Sara had had in mind, but they would have to do. On the upside, whether they were meant to be or not, they could be worn without stockings. And adding yet another layer to her already hot garments was not enticing.

When she reached the kitchen, Benedict hadn't returned from the Arsenale yet. Good. She would make him breakfast. But what did he have that she could prepare?

When he'd fixed their supper of cold ham and bread the previous evening, he'd taken the ham and bread from a small pantry off the kitchen. The salt-cured ham could be kept at room temperature. The pantry also contained jars and crocks of preserved food, bottles of wine, olive oil and vinegar, as well as a basket of potatoes. But he had gone outside for the butter. There was a well with a hand pump on it that was his source of water. However, to one side of the base of the pump was a round iron plate, for all the world like a small manhole cover. He lifted that plate and attached to the underside was a rope. He pulled the rope up and on the end of it was a very large covered basket, inside of which was a bottle of milk, a wheel of cheese, a container of butter, and another one of eggs. Clearly, the basket was lowered deep enough into the well to keep the contents cooler, without actually submersing them.

She went outside, pulled the basket up and took the butter, cheese, and two eggs from it before putting it back down the well. She'd make ham, eggs, fried potatoes, and bread.

She'd have loved to make biscuits or soda bread, but baking soda hadn't been invented yet and there was no oven chamber in the stove. However, yesterday he'd shown her the brick bread oven built outside, well away from the house. It hadn't been used since his mother had left. He had flour in the pantry from which she could make a sourdough starter. If she could figure out how to use the brick oven, she could make bread in a few days.

She washed and sliced the potatoes, put them in a bowl and covered them with water. They needed to soak for a few minutes so she mixed the flour and water for the starter, covered it with a cloth, and put it on the hutch where the dishes were stored. Then she sliced some ham and cut it into small cubes, finely chopped a small piece of cheese, and cut a few slices of bread. She'd love it toasted, but she wasn't quite sure how to do that.

She turned her attention back to the potatoes. She dried them before frying them in a mixture of butter and olive oil. It was a bit tricky to cook on the top of the stove without being able to control the temperature, but she managed to avoid burning the potatoes, frying them just until they were tender, then removing them to a plate to cool. She would finish everything after he returned. She filled the kettle and put it on to heat, then stepped out the back door.

He'd mentioned a garden the previous evening, but she hadn't had a chance to see what grew there. To her delight, there was a plethora of vegetables that were just coming into season. She'd take a close look later, but for now, she pulled up a couple of small onions. Beyond the garden was an orchard, which she'd have to explore later, too. She returned to the kitchen, her mind already planning dinner.

She washed and chopped the onions before toying with making a pot of tea so that she could have a cup while she waited. But with no idea when he'd be home, the pot might go cold before he returned and she didn't want to be wasteful.

She needn't have worried. She heard him coming through the front door just as the water reached the boil. She poked her head into the hall. "Breakfast is almost ready."

"Breakfast?

"Yes. Breakfast. The delicious first meal of the day."

He smiled, a slightly puzzled look on his face, but followed her into the kitchen. He had a large package wrapped in paper under one arm that he laid on the table.

She poured water into the teapot, then set about finishing breakfast. She put the potatoes on to fry again, allowing them to become a little crispy before adding the ham and onions. In another pan, she fried the two eggs. She sprinkled cheese on the potato mixture, and when it had just begun to melt, she divided it onto two plates and topped each with a fried egg.

She put the plates on the table and poured tea before she sat down. "Do you normally ask a blessing?"

Again, he gave her a quizzical smile. "Yes, I do."

She folded her hands, bowed her head, and waited.

"Bless us O Lord, and these thy gifts which we are about to receive from Thy bounty, through Christ our Lord. Amen."

"Amen," she echoed. She broke her egg so that the yolk drizzled onto the potato mixture then took a bite. It was delicious.

He followed suit. His face split into a broad smile when the food hit his lips. "This is delicious."

"Thank you."

"Is this something you do often?"

"Make breakfast?"

"Yes."

"Of course, doesn't everyone?"

"No."

No? "What do you mean?"

"I mean, I have never eaten anything like this at any time of the day, much less in the morning. But now that I have, I fear I shall only want more."

She frowned. "You don't eat breakfast?"

"Well, I might have some bread and butter with my tea, but that's all."

Whoops. "Uh…I'm sorry. I just thought…I'm sorry, I shouldn't have—"

"Sara, I'm not upset. This is wonderful. I've just never had it before. It makes me wonder where you learned to cook like this."

She shrugged. *The Food Network*, didn't seem like a good answer. "I don't know." She figured it would be best to just change the subject. "What's in the package?"

"Dinner."

"Dinner?"

He chuckled. "Yes, dinner. The large delicious meal in the middle of the day."

She laughed. "I mean, what is it?"

"It's a fish. A sea bass that I picked up in the fish market before coming home."

"I love sea bass."

"Do you know how to cook it?"

"Of course, I do. You'll love it."

"I'm sure I will."

Chapter 6

Benedict had loved the sea bass that evening and that thrilled Sara. She'd always enjoyed cooking, but Mark was the only person she had cooked for in quite a while. It wasn't that he didn't like her cooking, he did. "Babe that was great" came on the heels of almost every meal. But she'd learned early on that he liked the basics. He wanted plain meat and potatoes, no-frills vegetables, and iceberg salad with bottled ranch dressing.

After she made beef wellington once, he said, "I'm a guy, Sarah., I like steak, pork chops, ham, ribs, and hamburgers. I don't mind shrimp once in a while and crab cakes are okay, but don't waste your time on fish or anything *froufrou*."

He'd eat potatoes nearly anyway she fixed them, but the only vegetables he liked were zucchini, yellow squash, broccoli, cauliflower, green beans, and corn and the only way he liked them was boiled or steamed, with no sauce. He didn't mind spaghetti once in a while, but only with meatballs and tomato sauce. And the one time she fixed a rice dish, he pushed it around on the place and asked, "Hey, could we throw a potato in the microwave?"

So, she saved her more adventurous menus for nights when she was cooking only for herself.

She went to bed Monday night thinking of all the things she could try making that Benedict might not only eat, but enjoy. She'd start tomorrow with western omelets. This was going to be great. After just one day of trying to live without modern technology, she was having a blast. This little adventure was turning out to have all of the elements required for her ideal fantasy vacation.

First, she was close to the sea. She had been to beaches from New England to Florida and it didn't matter where it was, she loved the shore. She had grown up in Maryland and she could be at a Maryland or Delaware beach in a few hours. But perhaps her best ocean memories were from her family vacations. And since the accident, it was the one place where she could go to feel connected to her family through those wonderful memories.

From the time she was a little girl, her family had spent two weeks every summer at "arrogantly shabby" Pawley's Island, South Carolina. Two weeks of body surfing, shell hunting, building sand castles with her little brother, or just relaxing in a hammock with a good book. She read her first romance novel there. It had been given to her by a girl named Paula, whose family was vacationing there, too. She also experienced her first real kiss there, as she walked along the beach one night with a local boy she'd gotten to know over the years.

So, the location of her fantasy vacation was perfect. But she also absolutely loved to cook, and as fate would have it, just outside the back door, she had access to the freshest ingredients possible. Figuring out how to cook on a woodstove had been a bit of a challenge but so far, she'd succeeded. And as an added bonus, there was someone on hand who seemed to like eating her creations.

Which brought her to the last feature of her perfect holiday fantasy, someone fantastic to share it with. Kind, thoughtful, and oh so handsome, she couldn't imagine spending this time with anyone more wonderful than Benedict…well except for Mark. But then, he didn't really like her "*froufrou*" cooking, plus he provided excellent source material for her next hero, so Benedict was perfect under present conditions.

A little voice deep within her whispered, *Benedict is perfect…period.* But she did everything possible to quiet that voice. *I'm in love with Mark. I have to go back to my own time and once I do, I have a fourteen-day cruise ahead of me and Mark is going to propose.*

She drifted off to sleep as she had for at least the last month, imagining the wonderful things she and Mark would do on the cruise. And yet, at some point in her dreams, the man at her side on the cruise became Benedict.

~ * ~

Sara woke the next morning to the crowing of a rooster.

A rooster? Her eyes popped open and she almost squealed with delight when she realized that she actually was still in eighteenth-century Venice, courtesy of the pocket watch. She jumped up, dressed, and hurried downstairs to start breakfast. By the time Benedict joined her, she had beaten the eggs, sliced some cheese, and was sautéing the chopped ham, onions, and green peppers.

"Breakfast again?" he asked, sounding hopeful.

"Yes. Eggs a different way today. I normally would have it with toasted bread, but I'm not sure how to do that."

He laughed. "You know how to cook an absolutely amazing sea bass, but you can't toast bread?"

She shrugged, realizing how silly that had sounded. "I guess that's one of my missing memories.

"No need to worry. I can handle making toast."

82

So, as Sara finished putting the omelets together, he sliced several pieces of bread and one at a time, speared them on a long fork and held them near the stove to toast.

Just like roasting marshmallows. I should have thought of that.

Benedict appeared to enjoy the omelet every bit as much as he had yesterday's meals.

After breakfast was done, he offered to show her around a bit more.

She went into raptures of delight when she got a better look at exactly what was growing in his garden. "Ooh, you have a lot of ripe peas. If you want, we can have those for supper, with some of that zucchini. And fresh tomatoes. Wow, they look gorgeous."

He smiled. "If you'd like, we can have chicken, too."

"I'd love that. Where will you get the chicken?"

He cocked his head to one side. "Where one normally finds chickens, in the chicken coop."

"You have a chicken coop?"

"Sara, you have cooked eggs two mornings in a row. Where do you think they come from?"

She actually hadn't given it much thought because the eggs were in the basket down the well. "I know where eggs come from. I just didn't realize you had chickens. I thought perhaps you'd bought them." Even as she said it, she remembered the crowing rooster that had awakened her and felt like a prime idiot.

To his credit, he didn't laugh at her. "No, I actually keep chickens, but in fairness, the coop is set back from the house a ways so you probably didn't see it yesterday. I'll show you."

He led her to the coop with its fenced in yard. Nearby was a small stone byer. "I keep the feed in here." He took the lid off of a barrel and removed a large wooden scoop full of cracked corn. Then he showed her how to feed the chickens and collect the eggs.

"How often do they lay eggs?" she asked.

"About one a day. As you know, I keep the ones I collect in the well. But on the first four days of a month, I mark the eggs with a charcoal 'X' and leave them in the nests. If the marked eggs haven't hatched by the end of the month, I throw them out. Usually, enough hatch that I keep a steady population so there is always a supply of fresh eggs and chicken to eat."

"I've never eaten such fresh eggs."

He laughed. "How do you know?"

She smiled and shrugged. "I just do."

"Do you know how to cook chicken as well as you do eggs and fish?"

"Yes, I do. There is just one tiny problem."

"What's that?"

"I've only ever prepared a chicken that was already...uh...dressed."

He chuckled. "Again, I'm not sure how you know that, but I'll be happy to provide you with a *dressed* chicken."

He also showed her his orchard and it was beyond her wildest dreams. She had expected to find apples and maybe pears, but there were cherries, plums, and apricots as well— and much of it was ripe.

"What do you do with all of this amazing fruit?"

"I eat it and I dry some of it, but I don't have the time to harvest and preserve it all, so I share a lot with the birds. My mother used to make jams, but I don't really know how to do that."

Sara didn't know how to dry fruit, although she'd love to learn. But she did know how to make jams and jellies. "I hate to see it go to waste. I know how to make jams. If you have plenty of sugar, and crocks or jars to put it in, oh, and beeswax to seal it with, I'll make some for you."

"I have all of those things."

Nothing to Lose

And so, Sara picked vegetables and fruit while Benedict dressed the chicken and hunted down the supplies she needed. Then she was in her element for the rest of the day. She started the chicken cooking. She seasoned it with garlic, rosemary, sage, salt, and pepper and browned it in a large iron pot she would have called a Dutch oven. Then she added white wine, covered it with the lid, and allowed it to roast on top of the stove.

She washed and prepared the fruit and crockery while the chicken roasted. She made sautéed zucchini, peas and onions in a cream sauce, and fresh sliced tomatoes to go with the chicken.

She had the most wonderful time pulling dinner together and felt no small sense of pride that she'd done it with only a wood-burning stove. The icing on the cake was Benedict's words of praise as they enjoyed the meal together.

After dinner, she spent the rest of the afternoon making jam while Benedict worked in his study. They had cold chicken and spinach salad for dinner and she surprised him with stirred custard over fresh apricots for dessert.

"Sara, I don't think I've had such delicious meals in years. No, what am I saying? I don't think I've ever had such delicious meals."

As she went to bed that night, she realized that as much fun as she found cooking to be, it was way more fun to cook for someone who loved it.

~ * ~

The next day, she made crepes for breakfast, then spent the morning making pasta. Dinner was pasta primavera and poached plums for dessert. That afternoon he took her for a walk on the beach to the north end of the Lido. They passed blackberry thickets on the way. "Oh Benedict, can we pick some? I love blackberries."

"Of course, we can."

They picked and ate several handfuls.

"There is nothing better than juicy blackberries still warm from the sun. They are one of my absolute favorite fruits." She gave him a cheeky smile. "And you know, my blackberry preserves are almost better than my apricot jam."

"Well, then, we'll come back tomorrow with baskets because I have to taste that."

The only thing she really didn't like about her current circumstances was the heat combined with the layers of clothes she wore. After the first day, she had stopped wearing more than one petticoat and she had no compunction about rolling up her sleeves. But as they walked at the water's edge, it was just too tempting. She kicked off her shoes, gathered up her skirts, and waded into the cool water.

"What are you doing?" Benedict asked, an amused expression on his face.

"Cooling off. Join me."

He looked as if he were considering it for a moment. But when he looked poised to decline the invitation, she laughed and splashed water at him with her feet. "Come on. It's lovely and cool."

"I think you're a very wicked lass," he said even as he pulled off his shoes and stockings and waded into the water with her.

From the north end of the island, she could look across the lagoon and see Venice. Until then, she'd become so engrossed with eighteenth-century life, she'd almost forgotten where she was. "I would really love to see Venice. Do you suppose we could go?"

His brows drew together. "Of course."

"Can we go tomorrow?"

"I thought you said your sourdough will be ready to make bread with tomorrow."

"Oh, that's right. You promised to show me how to use the bread oven."

So the subject dropped.

~ * ~

The next day she did learn to use the bread oven that stood well away from the house. It was easier than she'd expected. She prepared the dough and when it was on its second rise, he showed her how to build a fire in the chamber. When the thick layer of bricks surrounding the oven were hot to the touch on the outside, it was ready. He showed her how to rake out the burning coals. "Then you put the loaves in and the bread bakes as the oven cools."

Once the bread was in the oven, Benedict said, "I'm going down to the village. I get milk, butter, and cheese from a farmer there. I can also get fresh beef or fish if you prefer."

"Can you wait until the bread is out of the oven, so I can go with you?"

"No, Sara, I don't think that's a good idea. People will wonder who you are, and since we don't know why you feel you are in danger, we probably shouldn't make your presence here widely known."

This was a bit of a disappointment, but it made sense. "I understand. But you will take me into Venice soon?"

"Of course."

"Maybe tomorrow?"

"I'll think about it."

She let the subject drop, but the next evening, as they walked along the west side of the island overlooking the lagoon, she asked again. "Oh, Benedict, Venice at sunset is beautiful."

He nodded. "Yes, it is."

She didn't want to ask again, but looked at him expectantly, hoping he would take the hint, but he didn't say anything.

As much as she wanted to go to Venice, she didn't push. It had been five days of absolute perfection. She had learned so much about ordinary life in this era, her books would already be richer for it. Then, of course, simply spending time alone with Benedict had been amazing. She grew fonder of him as each day passed. And at some point during the week, she realized that she derived more joy from the fact that he loved her cooking than she did just from cooking alone, and that was saying something.

She also realized that she'd stopped thinking about her novel early on and that's what she was here for after all. But perhaps most surprising, was that she'd stopped thinking about Mark.

A little voice deep within her whispered, *maybe that isn't so unusual. Maybe you've stopped thinking about Mark and your writing because Benedict isn't meant to be the hero in your next book, but the romantic hero of your life.* No. She had to stop that line of thinking. She had made too many mistakes before by falling in love with the idea of love, and he had given her no signals that he thought of her as anything more than a houseguest.

Chapter 7

Saturday arrived and after a wonderful breakfast of something Sara called "French Toast" with fresh blackberries, Benedict sequestered himself in his study to finish the plans for the new ship he'd been half working on all week. But once again, he couldn't quite focus. His mind kept drifting to Sara.

He had never met anyone like her and he'd never eaten so well in his life. His mother's hatred of all things Venetian also extended to the cuisine. She cooked the food that reminded her of her home and childhood. Her menus were plain but wholesome with little variation. Meat, potatoes, and boiled vegetables. Thus after she returned to Scotland and he was left to fend for himself, the only foods he knew how to cook were those he'd grown up with. His meals consisted mostly of pan fried fish or meat, and potatoes. Over the years, he had grown to love the fresh vegetables that grew so beautifully here and he cooked them to the best of his ability, but that was the extent of his variety.

Some of what Sara cooked was completely new to him, as the potatoes, ham, and eggs had been. But other dishes would have been served in any of the finest homes or establishments in Venice. He wondered how she could forget her very identity, but not this culinary artistry.

After barely one week, he knew he was beginning to fall in love with this beautiful girl from nowhere. His growing feelings weren't only because of her great skill in the kitchen, although that was certainly a gift. Over the week as he showed her around the north end of the Lido, he had become enchanted by her sheer enthusiasm for everything. She took such joy in each new discovery, ripe cherries, plums, and apricots in the orchard; peas, beans, tomatoes, cucumbers, chard, spinach, and melons in his garden; and wild blackberries thickets at the center of the island. Even something as ordinary as searching for eggs in the chicken coop was an adventure for her.

After her ordeal, he thought she might be afraid of the water, but he was wrong. He smiled as he remembered the afternoon she'd joyously kicked off her shoes, lifted her skirts scandalously high, and run knee deep into the sea, splashing water at him with her feet.

Perhaps he'd become jaded. The only women he encountered on a regular basis were those who worked as laborers in the shipyards, beaten down with their mundane existence. Or the women who sometimes accompanied a wealthy client. They were the polished courtesans whose elegant façades and practiced perfection never slipped for an instant.

But Sara, exuberant, ebullient, beautiful Sara, was as delightfully refreshing as a cool, fresh breeze on a blistering August day.

The one thing he hadn't done with her was take her into Venice.

She wanted to go. She'd asked several times and she'd stare across the lagoon wistfully but so far, he'd made excuses not to.

He wasn't sure exactly why but he didn't want to. He intended to take her...just not yet. Since she had arrived, they'd existed in their own world, away from other people. He had limited their wanderings to the unpopulated north end of the island, avoiding the village of Malamoco, altogether. Other than the farmer from whom he'd purchased butter, milk, and cheese, he hadn't seen or spoken to another person since he'd returned from the Arsenale on Monday morning. It was as if a delightful enchantment had woven itself around them, which only became stronger as each day passed. And yet, he knew with certainty, the enchantment would break the moment other people entered it.

So, he had jealously kept her to himself for as long as possible. But the time was coming. They couldn't stay secreted away forever. Still, there was one last thing he wanted to experience with her before the magic ended. On Saturday evening, she was putting the kitchen to rights after they'd eaten a supper of soup and fresh baked bread. He lit a lantern and went to the kitchen. She was sweeping the floor and he watched her for a moment from the door. He adored her. He simply couldn't explain it, but deep down, he believed she was meant for him.

She looked up and smiled at him. "I'm just finishing up."

He smiled back. "Good. Because I want to show you something." He held out his hand. "Come with me."

She nodded eagerly, put the broom by the hearth, and removed her apron. "Where are we going?"

"It's a surprise."

They chatted as they walked to the west side of the island.

When the twinkling lights of Venice came into view, she stopped and sighed, enraptured. "We've never been here at night. It's beautiful. Thank you, Benedict."

"Well I'm glad you find it beautiful, but that isn't all I planned for you to see."

"No?"

He grinned and shook his head. "No." Because the things she remembered and those she didn't were seemingly random, he asked, "Do you know what tomorrow is?"

She shook her head. "No."

"It's the third Sunday in July, the feast of the Most Holy Redeemer, *il Redentore*."

"Oh."

He laughed. "You don't know what that is."

Even in the lantern light, he could see a blush warm her cheeks as she smiled. "No, I don't."

"Well, almost two hundred years ago, in the year 1577, a great plague gripped the city. More than fifty thousand people died. Have you ever heard of the artist, Titian? No, I don't suppose you'd remember even if you had, but he was among those who died. The Doge at the time promised to build a magnificent church if Venice was freed from that plague. So, when it eventually did end, he commissioned the Church of the Most Holy Redeemer to be built. Look across the water, you can see the Campanile di San Marco, the cathedral tower?"

"Yes."

"Now, look to the left. Can you see the long narrow island across from San Marco?"

"Yes."

"That is the Giudecca and it's where the church was built. First, they laid a foundation stone over which they built a small wooden church. There was also a temporary bridge, created from barges so that the Doge could lead a procession across the water to the tabernacle. Since then, the Doge has made that same procession every year. After Mass is said there is a great celebration throughout Venice. And festivals in Venice are not to be missed."

She clasped her hands together. "You'll take me?"

Her unbridled excitement at the prospect was endearing. He couldn't have said "no" if he'd wanted to. But he didn't want to. He wanted to show her a Venice as full of life as she was.

"Yes, I will."

"Oh, Benedict, thank you." She threw her arms around him in a jubilant hug. "I can't wait. What should I wear? I don't think I'll be able to sleep tonight, but I should probably try. Maybe we should go back now." She took a step towards the path home.

He put a hand out to stop her, chuckling at her childlike joy. "In a few minutes. But there's something else I want you to see."

Nothing to Lose

Almost as if on cue, a firework exploded over the lagoon.

"Fireworks?" she said in awe.

He nodded. "Aye. There's always a display or fireworks on the evening before *il Redentore.*

~ * ~

As Sara watched the fireworks explode over eighteenth century Venice, she felt like she should pinch herself. This couldn't be happening. It had to be a dream. But if it was, the entire week had been. Perhaps the stirring in her belly that she was beginning to feel every time Benedict complimented her cooking, or took her to experience something new…or just sat across the table from her, was part of the dream too.

But she knew it wasn't.

She was falling for Benedict, and that was a disaster waiting to happen. She had to go home. There was a man waiting for her who loved her. *And let you go to bed alone while he stayed in the casino to gamble. Just imagine what it would be like for Benedict to take you in his arms and kiss you senseless.*

No, she had to stop this. She had to channel these romantic thoughts about Benedict into Rafe, the hero of her work in progress. And blond-haired, blue-eyed Kyra was the woman he loved.

She imagined Rafe and Kyra sitting on the rocks watching the fireworks. *He cupped Sara's cheeks in his hands, gently tilting her head as he lowered his lips to meet hers.*

~ * ~

Sara found the trip to Venice the next day nothing short of magical.

Benedict had urged her to wear a pale-blue silk damask, close-bodied gown, the style of which Sara recognized as *robe à l'anglaise.*

"Are you sure it's appropriate?" Sara knew there were sumptuary laws in much of Europe in the eighteenth century that would prevent a commoner from dressing in such finery. "You said you weren't a nobleman and I'm certainly not a member of the gentry. Is it acceptable for me to wear this?"

"Maybe you are a member of the nobility. You might be a British earl's daughter for all we know."

"I'm pretty confident I'm not."

"Well, it's of no importance anyway. Wealth matters in Venice nearly as much as title does. Here, the attire of affluent merchants and businessmen is not restricted by sumptuary laws."

"Yes, but I'm not affluent."

"For someone with no memories, you are overly certain of things. The shift you were wearing when I found you was made of silk. Besides, you will be with me."

She didn't offer any further argument. She truly did want to wear the beautiful dress. She didn't have a corset, but the gown fit beautifully without it. Still, once she had it on, she realized that the dress revealed a fairly large portion of her décolletage. She looked among Mrs. MacIan's things for a *fichu*, a little kerchief that women wore around their neck that tucked into the bodice of a dress to make it more modest. But it was to no avail.

Just own it, Sara, she told herself. She went downstairs, head up, appearing as confident as she could until Benedict saw her.

His mouth fell open and she felt a hot blush rise. Her hand fluttered to her neck, trying to conceal what felt like an acre of exposed skin.

"Sara, you are breathtaking."

"Thank you, but I feel…I feel…well, the neckline is a bit low. I couldn't find a *fichu*."

"My mother probably didn't leave one. And the neckline isn't too low by Venetian standards. But I did find this in a trunk." He handed her a beautiful lace shawl. "It's Burano lace." He gave her a sad smile. "Another gift from my father that my mother rejected."

Sara took it reverently in her hands. "It's simply gorgeous."

"I thought you might want to wear it on your head. I don't have any hats or head coverings of any sort left of hers. And it will provide a little extra coverage."

Benedict himself looked rather sharp. Since she'd arrived, she'd only seen him dressed in breeches, boots, and a shirt. Now he wore a suit, complete with stockings, shoes with silver buckles, and a tricorn hat. He looked very much the gentleman.

They walked to the small dock where Benedict had two boats moored, a batela and a gondola. Surprisingly, the black, flat-bottomed gondola looked much like those still used in Venice. The batela was a slightly larger flat-bottomed sailboat that could also be rowed.

"If the wind is right, it's much faster to sail across the lagoon and if I'm just going to the shipyard, it is what I nearly always use. It takes between twenty and thirty minutes to row across the lagoon, depending on conditions, but the gondola is easier to maneuver within the canals. Today, we'll use it."

He helped settle her into the *felze*, the gondola's cabin, before handing her his coat and hat. "Would you mind holding these? It's much easier to row without being constricted by a dress jacket."

He took his place, standing on the back of the gondola, pushed off from the dock, and began rowing them across the lagoon.

It was breathtakingly romantic. She imagined Rafe and Kyra doing the same thing only in an open gondola, like the ones in Venice now. She tried to imagine their conversation. But after a few moments, she mentally set the novel aside. She wanted to enjoy this ride herself.

~ * ~

That afternoon and evening, as they wandered the familiar streets of Venice, Benedict felt as if he were seeing them for the first time. He guessed, in a sense, it was like a first time, because he was seeing it all through her sharp eyes. Something new, things that he normally took no notice of, caught her attention every few hundred yards. The windows of bookstores and tailors' shops, the food vendors, puppet shows, and street performers enthralled and delighted her. Even just watching the other people around them while they had coffee at a café on San Marco Square was rich entertainment for her.

As the hour grew late, and the revelers more raucous, Sara clearly grew weary. Benedict guided her away from San Marco square and in no time, they were back at the place where he had moored the gondola.

"Are we leaving?" she asked.

"Aye. Things will only get wilder as the night goes on. It isn't the place for an innocent young lady. Besides, you are already over-tired."

"I'm not," she said, even as she stifled a yawn.

"I beg to differ. But even if you aren't tired, I am. Tomorrow I will need to go to the shipyard. As much as I would like to stay with you, I can't ignore my business."

"I'm sorry, Benedict. Of course, you can't. Yes, I suppose it is time to go home."

Home.

She had said the word.

All week she had referred to it as *his house* or *the house*.

But just now she had called it *home*. Perhaps she, too, was beginning to imagine spending the rest of her life with him.

Chapter 8

Eighteenth century Venice was everything Sara had imagined it to be and so much more. She simply wanted to soak it all in, fix it in her brain forever. These memories, made without a single video or photograph, were going to have to last her a lifetime. She went to bed that night with all the sights, sounds, and smells swirling in her head. She smiled to herself, remembering the scene from *My Fair Lady* after Eliza Doolittle came home from the ball singing "I Could Have Danced All Night". Except that she hadn't been dancing at a ball, it was exactly how Sara felt.

But Benedict had been right when he observed that she was tired. She was asleep before she could finish humming the show tune.

She heard the cock crow before daylight the next morning. Part of her wanted to sleep just a little longer and she rolled over, covering her head with a pillow. Then she remembered that Benedict was going to the shipyard today. She wouldn't see him until tonight if she went back to sleep.

She scrambled out of bed, dressed, and hurried out of her room just as he was leaving his.

"Sara, it's dreadfully early. You don't need to get up. Go back to bed for a while."

"I'll do no such thing. I want you to have a good breakfast before you leave."

He grinned. "I won't lie, I've become quite fond of your breakfasts."

"Good. It won't take long." She hurried down the steps ahead of him and out into the yard to the well to retrieve the butter and eggs. He had a kettle of water heating before she returned from the yard.

Last week, he had shown her how to toast bread using a toasting fork and she had made a small batch of apricot preserves. So, she served him ham and eggs with toast and jam before walking with him to the dock just as dawn was gilding the sky.

"The shipyards, all industry really, close down for about two hours in the middle of the day so people can have their dinner. I have been in the habit of eating my main meal of the day then, at a cafe in town."

"Oh." This disappointed Sara. She had grown to love mealtimes with him.

"But," he continued, "if it's all right with you, I think I'll grab something small and work through the dinner break so I can come home and have a later dinner with you."

She beamed at him. "I'd love that."

"Shall I bring some fresh meat or fish?"

"Not today. I have something already planned."

"Then I should see you by about six this evening."

"See you then."

He climbed into the batela, pushed off from the dock, and waved to her.

She watched until he was well on his way before returning to the house. She did have plans today. Lots of them.

She'd start by doing laundry. Benedict had told her he paid a lady in the village to do his washing. But she had decided, as long as she was here, she would take care of this. It was the least she could do to repay his kindness.

By midday she'd drawn and heated water repeatedly, washed all of the dirty clothes and towels and hung them to dry, removed the linens from the beds and washed and hung them. When she stopped to make lunch, she smiled. In the twenty-first century, she'd be taking a break from writing about now to go to the gym. There was absolutely no need for a gym in this time. Just doing laundry had been a total body workout.

After lunch, she took a bucket to the lagoon side of the island, where she'd seen mussels clinging to the rocks.

The tide was out so it would be easy to find and gather them. She pulled the back of her skirt between her legs and tucked it into her apron in the front to keep her skirt out of the water as she waded around the rocks, plucking the largest mussels until she had a bucketful.

Tonight's dinner would be mussels sautéed with garlic, scallions, olive oil, and white wine, served with fried polenta and a ragout of chard and tomato. It would be ages before Benedict returned home, but the mussels needed to rest in a bucket of sea water for several hours to spit out all of the sand they held.

After she returned home, she would take a break from working and think about the plot for her novel. She imagined Kyra stepping through the portal to the eighteenth century. Perhaps she was dressed in period clothing on her way to a masquerade. She doesn't know what to do or where to go and she can't get back through the portal. Finding a beautiful woman alone, several men set upon her, when Rafe di Santi comes out of nowhere, brandishing his sword and sending the brigands on their way.

Yes, that was a good start.

~ * ~

Nothing to Lose

When Benedict reached the shipyard that morning, a number of issues were waiting for his attention.

Emilio poked his head into Benedict's office shortly after noon. "Ah, mountains of paperwork is the price one pays for a week of leisure."

"Not exactly leisure. I completed the new design." He handed his partners the drawings, on which he'd worked all week—when he could pry himself away from his houseguest for a few minutes.

Emilio stretched the drawings out over a large table to look at them. "These are excellent, Benedict. Very beautiful. Absolutely inspired."

Benedict grinned at Emilio's innocent choice of words. He had indeed been inspired by a great beauty. "Thank you."

"Come, take a break and have dinner with me. I can fill you in on all of the latest news."

"Actually, Emilio, I was hoping to leave before five this evening, so I thought I'd just take a quick break and stay working. Besides, not much could have happened in a week."

"Ah, you'd be surprised. Do you remember Reese Llewellyn?"

"How could I forget him? One of the most obnoxious Welshman ever to walk the earth."

Emilio chuckled. "That's the one. Wants the biggest and best of everything for the handful of *soldi* in his pocket."

"Has he commissioned another ship that he doesn't want to pay for?"

Emilio sobered. "No. In fact it is truly a tragic set of events. Llewellyn has a daughter who fancied herself an artist and wanted to come to Venice to study. Unbeknownst to him, she'd even hired a tutor to teach her Venetian. But apparently, when she asked her father to bring her here, he patently refused. So the girl, clearly cut from the same stubborn bolt as her father, defied him and booked passage here accompanied only by a maidservant."

"Who would have allowed two unaccompanied young women to book passage?"

"Apparently his nineteen-year-old daughter disguised herself as a widow. Heavily veiled as she was, and speaking Venetian, no one questioned her. But as soon as he learned of the girl's rash act, he set out in his fastest ship. The one, incidentally, we built for him."

"That he thought wasn't worth the price we charged?"

"The very one. And even though it was several days before he knew what his daughter had done, he was able to overtake the ship she was on shortly before they reached port here."

"So, he caught his errant daughter and took her home? I'm sure the girl wasn't happy, but in the grand scheme of things that hardly seems tragic."

"Sadly, his daughter wasn't on board the ship when he reached it. According to her maid servant, the daft girl jumped overboard to avoid her father's wrath."

Benedict's heart nearly stopped at those words. "Jumped overboard? Did she drown?"

"Everyone assumes she did. The maid saw her go under and never surface. But the next day, some of the clothes the foolish girl had been wearing were found, but her body wasn't."

"He thinks she's alive?"

"Yes, he clings to that hope. He's sent men to all the islands to see if she could possibly have been plucked from the water by someone and taken to safety."

"I see. What was…I mean, do you know anything about her? What she looks like? Her name?"

"She's apparently a pretty little thing. Dark hair, fair skin, blue eyes, and her name is Ceres."

Benedict's mouth went dry. "Well that is…uh…tragic. I will make inquiries at Malamoco when I return home this evening."

"I'm sure Llewellyn will appreciate that. He is, well there's no other word for it, *distraught*. She's his only child and he has most likely lost her forever."

Benedict could only nod.

"Now, if you're sure you won't dine with me, I'll leave you to your work."

"I'm sure

"Enjoy your dinner."

Benedict simply stared at the closed door after Emilio had left. He had been right about the enchantment breaking. His beautiful sea nymph was not Sara, the girl from nowhere. She was Ceres Llewellyn, the daughter of an odious man. A man who Bendedict neither liked nor respected. The man was apparently distraught, searching frantically for his wayward daughter when all the time, she had been with Benedict, secluded at the north end of the Lido. Had she lied to him the entire time?

No, he refused to believe that. He was certain Sara had no clue who she really was.

Benedict knew that he should seek the man out and tell him his daughter was safe, ease his mind. But something in him couldn't. The only thing Sara seemed to remember was her profound fear. He couldn't go speak with Llewellyn until after he'd talked to her.

He tried to focus on his work for the rest of the afternoon, but with Ceres Llewellyn on his mind, he accomplished nothing. He finally gave up and sailed back across the lagoon.

Chapter 9

Benedict had never dreaded something so much in his life. He was about to lose the beautiful girl he was growing to love. When he stepped inside his home, the heavenly aroma from the kitchen reminded him of everything that he had come to love about her and would miss so terribly if she returned to England with her father.

Before he could make himself take the first step towards the kitchen, she came through the door. "Benedict, you're home. I've missed you today, but wait until you see what I've fixed for dinner."

Holy Mother of God. Could coming home to a wife be better than this? Could he desire anything more?

Then it occurred to him. He could marry her. Why not? He could simply speak to her father once she'd returned to him. After all, Llewellyn wasn't a nobleman. He was a merchant, a businessman. Benedict was a partner in an extremely successful business himself. There were no class issues here. That thought cheered him. Maybe this wasn't such a bad thing after all. When dinner was over, he would tell her everything.

And once again, dinner was a masterpiece. Now that he knew who she was, it was hard to imagine how she had learned to cook like this. Surely as Reese Llewellyn's cosseted only child, she had never had to prepare a meal. But then again, this was the girl who hired a tutor behind her father's back so she could learn to speak Venetian. Anything was possible.

After dinner, he helped her wash up. She tried to chivy him out of the kitchen, but he wouldn't be dissuaded. He needed to talk to her and didn't want to prolong the agony.

When the kitchen had been set to rights, he took her hand. "Sara, come with me to the sitting room. There is something I want to talk with you about."

"This seems very serious."

"It is serious."

She frowned but went along, taking the chair opposite him. "What's wrong?"

"I learned some news today that you need to hear. A man, a fairly well known British merchant who is a client of Santi and MacIan, has been searching all over Venice for his daughter."

"No."

Benedict nodded. "Yes, Sara. Apparently his nineteen-year-old daughter wanted to come to Venice. When he wouldn't allow it, she came anyway with a maidservant. Llewellyn followed in a faster ship, and when he was about to overtake the one on which she sailed, she jumped overboard."

Sara's face went ashen. "Maybe she drowned."

"Maybe, but they only found her clothes. Not her body."

Sara nodded. "I see."

"I think you are his missing daughter."

"So, it would seem."

"Her name…your name…is Ceres Llewellyn."

"And you've told her father I'm here?"

"Not yet. I knew you were afraid and I wanted to talk to you first."

She sighed heavily, obviously relieved. "Thank goodness."

"But, Ceres, I need to take you to him tomorrow."

"I don't want you do that."

Frankly, he didn't want to do it either. "I must. It is the right thing. He is apparently distraught over losing you."

"No, Benedict, you can't tell him I'm here and you can't take me to him."

The fear in her voice gutted him. "Why not?"

"I have a bad feeling about it. A really bad feeling. I'm certain it's a mistake."

"I'm sorry, Ceres, that's not good enough."

She nodded, sighed, and looked him directly in the eye. "You can't take me to him, because I'm not Ceres."

"Sweetheart, you know you are."

"No, I'm not. But it's a long story. Please listen to the whole thing before you pass any judgment."

"All right. I'll listen."

"My name is not Ceres Llewellyn. It's Sara Wells."

"Wait, were you her servant? Did the two of you switch places?" This could resolve everything.

"No, Benedict. What I'm about to tell you is hard to believe because it belies a truth that you, in fact most people, have believed their entire lives. That time flows only in one direction."

"Because it does."

"Generally, yes. But it is possible for someone from the future to travel back in time and vice-versa."

Benedict was stunned. "You don't seriously expect me to believe that."

"I do because it's true. But you said you'd listen to the whole story."

"So I did." Benedict wasn't sure whether Ceres had been lying to him the whole time and was attempting to perpetuate the lie, or whether she was simply ill, but he would listen.

Ceres slipped a hand into the neck of her dress, grasped the gold pendant that she was wearing when he found her, and pulled it up and over her head. She opened the cover to reveal not a locket, as he had assumed, but a pocket watch. "This watch was given to me by an old woman named Gertrude. The story she told me was absolutely impossible. She said that if I put it around my neck and told it a special word before I went to sleep at night, I would wake up in some other time. *In someone else's body.* I didn't really believe it. I mean who would? But somehow the more I talked to her, the more I believed it would work—or at least I'd regret forever not trying it. So, I accepted the watch and did what she told me to."

The story Ceres told was absolutely preposterous. She wanted him to believe that she was Sara Wells, a twenty-seven-year-old American woman from the twenty-first century who had exchanged souls with Ceres Llewellyn for sixty days. It was simply outrageous. But as she answered his questions, providing remarkable detail, he began wonder if it could be true.

How could she be making this up? He looked into her eyes as she explained things. She appeared guileless, and sincerely believed what she was telling him. And she clearly hadn't taken leave of her senses. Thus, there was only one explanation. She was exactly who she said she was, a soul from over two hundred years in the future who could only stay fifty-two more days. That fact nearly shattered him.

Dear God, I'm going to lose her. More assuredly than if she had been Ceres.

He had come to love her. He'd allowed himself to hope she would marry him and stay with him forever. But that couldn't happen.

He sighed and turned away from her. "Why did you decide to do this?"

"Benedict, if someone offered you the chance to see another time, if they told you you'd only be away from your own body for a minute and the only thing you had to do for it to happen was say a word and go to sleep, would you try it?"

He didn't even have to think about it. He'd accept in the space of a heartbeat if there was a chance it would take him to her. "Yes."

"You see? It's as I said, I feared regretting it forever if I didn't try it."

"What did you hope to find?"

Her face lit with the enthusiasm he had come to love. "This." She spread her arms wide. "All of this. The chance to simply experience life in another time. I'm an author. I write love stories. A few of them have been set in the past. History fascinates me. I think it fascinates a lot of people because more and more books are being written about time travel."

"I suppose so if it's possible."

"But it isn't possible. What I mean is, most people believe it isn't possible. I thought it wasn't possible. Still, it's an intriguing idea. I thought how amazing it would be to write a time travel story, having actually travelled through time."

"And you picked eighteenth century Venice?"

"I had no choice in the matter. I didn't know where I would end up, but it didn't matter. I just wanted to see what another time was really like. I could scarcely believe that I'd arrived in Venice. I had been in Venice just the previous day. It is still one of the most beautiful and romantic cities in the world."

"So, you will use your experiences here to write a book?"

"Yes, I plan to. I even have an idea about how to accomplish the time-travel element."

He cocked his head to one side. "Well that seems obvious. The pocket watch."

"No. I can't use the pocket watch. No one would believe the whole soul exchange thing, and it's terribly hard to explain. I'm going to have a time portal."

He couldn't suppress a smile. "That's more believable? Have you ever encountered a time portal?"

"No."

"But you are here because of a pocket watch?"

"Yes."

"But a time portal in more believable?"

She laughed. "I suppose it sounds silly, but yes. I think simply walking, body and soul, through a door in time will be easier to accept than people's souls trading places."

"I don't know why. Souls enter and leave bodies every day. Outside of a body a soul exists in nothingness and can cross the threshold of heaven, hell, and purgatory. Why shouldn't it be able to cross through time?"

"Then you believe me?"

He nodded. "I do."

"Thank you. I…well…thank you. So, now you see why we can't tell Ceres's father."

"I believe that you exchanged souls with Ceres, but you can still experience this time and let Ceres's father know she's alive."

"But she isn't. Not really. She was meant to die. She made a choice that would have led to her certain death and when I leave, she will die. Maybe it's better not to put her father through this agony twice. Ceres is gone. She is truly gone. I'm not Ceres. What's more, even the thought of going to see her father fills me with dread. As I mentioned, Gertrude said some memories leak through. I am dead certain I need to avoid her father at all costs."

"Sara, my life here is isolated and if you stayed here that would be fine, but you won't experience much more of Venice if you do that. I also fear that your presence here won't go unnoticed forever, and it will eventually get back to your father. Even worse if you die here, I could be accused of murdering you."

"No, I've already thought of that and I won't let it happen. I have it all worked out. When the time comes, I will swim back into the Adriatic. Once I'm well away from this island, I will say the word. If Cere's body is ever found, it will be consistent with what everyone already believes happened. If not...well, it doesn't matter then."

"I suppose you're right. If you are going back maybe it is better to spare him a bit of pain." He furrowed his brow. "There is more to this soul exchange business than first meets the eye. Having to decide how and when someone dies can't be easy. While it seems like there's nothing to lose when you've been offered the chance to use the pocket watch, I'll warrant no one fully grasps the fact that they are having an impact on more than just themselves."

She nodded somberly. "I think that is very true." She was silent for a moment. "I know I probably shouldn't ask this, but can I stay here with you and explore Venice until it's time for me to leave?"

He wanted to say 'no,' to beg her to spare him the agony of seeing her every day, all the while knowing she could never be his. But he coveted the little time he had left with her and wouldn't turn his back on it. "Yes. You are welcome here."

"Oh, Benedict," she exclaimed jumping to her feet and hugging him. "This is wonderful and it'll be so much fun. I'm so glad you know about the pocket watch. There will be no secret between us. It will almost be like having a brother again."

She thought of him as a brother? Dear God, how much worse could this get? Then he realized exactly what she had said. "A brother again? Did something happen to him?"

~ * ~

Sara hadn't planned on having this conversation, but once her hand was forced she was very thankful that she did. It made the whole situation simpler, and he knew exactly where things stood before she did something foolish—like fall in love with him.

She liked Benedict. She liked him a lot. In fact, if she were being honest with herself, she was already falling in love with him, and she had to stop that at all costs. Unfortunately, the romantic in her wanted to love and be loved so much that she constantly misread signals from the men she had dated. She believed she had fallen in love before—several times. Each time she was certain that the magical happy ending was just ahead, only to have her heart broken.

Now she found herself in another time, in a romantic city, with an extraordinarily handsome man who could have stepped out of the pages of one of her books. If she made the same mistake this time, and worse, decided to stay because of it, it would be devastating. The fact that he didn't love her might be the least of her problems. And snuggling up with a pint of ice-cream and watching sappy movies until she had cried it all out, or whatever the eighteenth century equivalent of that was, wouldn't fix things.

Besides, hadn't she already fallen in love with Mark? Even as that thought occurred to her, it didn't feel exactly right. She couldn't quite put her finger on why.

Still, it didn't really matter. She needed to protect herself by keeping him firmly in the "friend" realm. She actually believed he could be "like a brother" to her until the words tumbled out of her mouth. She didn't feel remotely sisterly towards him.

"Sara, did you hear me?"

"I'm sorry, what?"

"You *had* a brother?"

Ugh. It still felt like a fist to her gut every time she thought about it. "Yes. He was eight years younger than me. But he and my parents were killed in a car accident."

"What's a car accident?"

"A car is like a carriage that doesn't require horses. It uses an engine that burns gas, but that technology won't be invented for about a hundred years. Anyway, by the middle of the twentieth century, they became very popular and very powerful. They can travel at high speeds. Three years ago, we had all been to a band concert at his school. He played the trumpet. I was in graduate school at the time and lived in an apartment near the university, so I had driven myself. They were on their way home and a girl who was going way too fast and not paying attention to what she was doing drifted into their lane. Apparently, Dad swerved to miss her, spun out, and tumbled down an embankment."

"And they were killed?"

"Not instantly." Tears welled in her eyes. "My dad died within a few hours, but Mom and Josh were severely injured. Mom died after three days. Josh lived for eight more days after that."

He put his arms around her. "Oh, Sara, I'm so sorry. Do you have any other family?"

"No. It's just me now." She rested her head against his chest and it felt oh, so good. Mark had never done this. She hadn't met him yet when the accident occurred and if the subject arose, he rushed to change it to something less distressing. But she knew Benedict had suffered a similar loss. He understood.

"I know what it's like to be alone. It must have been hard for you. It must be hard still."

She nodded. "As time passes, it has gotten a little easier. The pain is still there, just not as sharp and intense."

"Aye, it's the same for me." He kissed the top of her head. "I fear that pain will never go away completely, but we'll grow stronger with time."

No one had comforted her like this in a long time. But as much as she longed for it, if she gave in and allowed herself to love him, she'd have another loved one to mourn the loss of in a few weeks.

She stepped back, wiped her eyes and took a deep breath. "Thank you, Benedict. It's been a busy day, and I'm bone weary. I'll tell you more about the twenty-first century tomorrow but for now, I think I'll bid you goodnight and find my bed.

He nodded. "Goodnight, Sara."

"Goodnight." She practically fled from the room and up the stairs.

Chapter 10

Sara had been tired. It was the good, satisfied kind of tired that signals a day where much has been accomplished. In addition to the laundry, she had dusted and swept the bedrooms before remaking the beds with the freshly laundered linens.

The rest of the laundry was a little daunting. Everything needed to be ironed. She knew that Benedict had someone else do his laundry, but surely his mother had had irons. Sara searched until she found them, shoved way to the back, on the bottom shelf in the pantry. They were black cast iron. She'd seen similar in antique shops and knew enough from old pictures to get the gist of how they were used. She put them on the stove to heat.

She couldn't find anything that looked like an ironing board, but she'd made do by putting towels on the kitchen worktable. She used one iron until it cooled then switched to the other one. She'd started with her own undergarments, figuring that if she fouled it up too badly, the damage wouldn't show. That was a good decision because, while she was now the proud owner of a scorched petticoat, she'd figured out that the fabric needed to be damp. The task took hours but allowed her lots of time to plan more of her new book. With no one in the house to hear her, she tried out bits of dialogue. She even decided on the title: *The Passageway*.

When she was done, it was time to fix supper. When the last pot was dried, she was tired, but very proud of all she'd accomplished.

Then Benedict had told her about Ceres.

Now Sara lay in bed, her mind whirling with the consequences of having exchanged souls with someone.

Last week the entire experience had been a lark. Sara had been having a wonderful time and had even likened it all to a fantasy vacation. But there was one big flaw in that. When one went home after a brilliant vacation, new friends were not lost forever, no one died and no one was left to mourn a lost loved one.

She had convinced herself that because neither she nor Benedict knew who she was, she was actually just herself. But she wasn't. She resided in Ceres Llewellyn's body and the only thing she knew about the girl was that she wanted to avoid her father.

Then, too, Sara had convinced herself that Benedict was simply the source material for her next hero. But he wasn't. He was a living, breathing, eighteenth century man who had been nothing but kind to her. But now he would have to deal with the consequences of her imminent death.

Perhaps she shouldn't have asked him to let her stay. Perhaps she should have just asked him to take her to Venice. She could have figured out some way to get by…at least for a few days, if not the whole amount allotted. But she couldn't bear the thought of that. The time she spent with him was nothing short of magical. She didn't want to give that up yet. She also didn't want love to get mixed up in this whole mess. Furthermore, she'd accepted the watch so she could research this time and place. So she vowed to stay focused and avoid falling in love at all costs.

Eventually she fell asleep but her rest was disturbed by dreams she didn't understand. She woke the next morning, still tired, but she got up and dressed quickly anyway. She wanted to see Benedict before he left for the Shipyard.

She had stoked the fire and had the kettle boiling before he came downstairs.

"You're up early."

"A little, but I didn't want to miss you this morning."

He frowned. "You look tired. You don't have to wake before I leave. I'm perfectly capable of making myself tea."

"I know you are, but I do like making meals for you."

"I like that too. And I like fresh linens on the bed. I didn't realize that you'd done the laundry until I went up for the night. Thank you."

"You're welcome. You've provided me a home. It's the least I can do."

"Still, I don't want you to wear yourself out. Go back to bed for a while now and get some more rest."

"I couldn't sleep if I tried and I don't want to. I wanted to ask you something."

"Ask away."

"I'd like for you to take me to Venice today."

"I'd love to, but I really have to work. We'll go again on Sunday."

"I know you have to work and I'm not asking for you to escort me. I thought I'd just wander around a bit and see what things are like. You know, just ordinary life."

"No, Sara. That is out of the question. You can't wander around Venice alone. It isn't safe."

"It's broad daylight. Nothing can happen."

"All kinds of things could happen. Young women do not wander around Venice alone. You might be mistaken for a courtesan or worse, a prostitute. You can go to Venice when I can stay with you. Not today."

"Maybe I could dress as a boy. No one would pay any attention to me then."

Benedict frowned.

"Please, Ben. I only have sixty days here, eight of which are gone. There are only seven Sundays left. That isn't nearly enough time. The whole sixty days isn't enough time. I can't waste it."

"I don't think it's a good idea. Even dressed as a boy something could happen to you."

"Will you at least think about it?"

He sighed. "Yes, I'll think about it."

Sara decided not to press him more. After he'd thought about it, she'd have another chance. "Thank you, Ben."

She fixed breakfast for him and packed a sandwich and fruit for his lunch. She smiled, thinking cookies were needed. She'd try to bake some today.

~ * ~

Benedict couldn't get Sara's request off his mind all day.

For that matter, he couldn't get anything about Sara off his mind. And every thought, every memory gouged at the spot in his heart he'd made for her that he now feared would be empty forever.

He forced himself to remember that she was simply here to learn. She had to leave. Maybe he should let her do as she wished. He had no authority over her.

But what if something happened to her? He'd never forgive himself.

And so, the circular argument with himself continued incessantly until the workday was over. By which time he'd accomplished little. He sailed across the lagoon and still hadn't made a decision by the time he walked up to the house from the dock. Seeing the light shining from the kitchen caused his heart to ache afresh. She had become a light in his life. He had let himself imagine this, coming home every day for the rest of his life, to Sara.

As she had the previous day, Sara had prepared a wonderful meal. She didn't raise the subject of going to Venice during dinner and he'd half hoped she'd changed her mind or forgotten it. But that was a vain hope.

After dinner, she poured them both a cup of tea and put a plate of something she called *snickerdoodles* on the table between them.

"Ben, have you thought any more about me spending time in Venice?"

Ben. She'd started calling him that and he liked it. "It seems I've thought of nothing but that today. Sara, it just isn't safe."

"Even as a boy?"

"Even as a boy."

She turned her head away, clearly frustrated. "I think you are taking this too seriously."

"It's your life I'm worried about. I don't think it's possible to take that too seriously."

Looking directly at him again, she said, "I am smart and resourceful. I think I can manage to stay out of trouble. But the truth is, I am going to die anyway. If I get into a bad spot and push comes to shove, I can always say the return word and go home early."

That thought tore at his heart. He didn't want her to go home early. He didn't want her to go at all. "If you do that, you won't even have your seven Sundays."

"That's a risk I'm willing to take."

But I'm not. He looked into her eyes, so beautiful and so full of determination. As much as he wanted to, he could not keep her locked away here. Although she'd be safe, she wouldn't be happy. She wasn't here to be his wife. She was here to learn and return to her own time. "Fine."

"Then I can go tomorrow?"

133

"Not tomorrow. I do think it will be safer for you to be dressed as a boy and that'll take some work. My mother didn't like to throw anything away. She packed a lot of old things in the attic, believing they might come in handy someday. There might be old shoes there. She also kept a box that she put worn out clothes in to use for rags or patches and the like. I think it's in the attic. I expect we'll be able to find something that I outgrew in that. But you'll need to alter anything we find in order to make it fit. And I suspect you'll need to do some repairs as well. If you can put together an adequate costume by tomorrow, I'll take you into Venice on Thursday."

"The attic? Can we go look now?"

"If you wish."

He took a lamp and guided her up the narrow stairs that led to the attic from the second floor. He located the box and together they went through it. He did find a pair of breeches with worn out knees and a crumpled, stained shirt that had probably been his when he was fifteen or so. Both were much too big and would take some work to be presentable. He also located a trunk containing several old pairs of shoes that had been his through the years. Sara was able to find a pair that fit relatively well. "You'll need a hat too. I have one downstairs that is a little worn. It may be a little too big, but since you'll need to tuck your hair up into it anyway, so I expect it will fit. You can use your own stockings."

She grinned. "This is all great. I'll work on it tomorrow."

Unable to match her enthusiasm, he just nodded.

"Ben, I know you're worried, but I'm sure nothing will happen. I'll just experience everyday life and at the end of the day, I'll make my way back to the Arsenale in time to come home with you."

Home. Maybe if she thought of it as home, she'd decide not to leave. Perhaps it too was a vain hope, but he needed something to hold onto if he was going to make it through the next fifty some days.

Chapter 11

The next day Sara worked for hours on her boy clothes. She put a pot of soup on in the afternoon, so she could keep working and finish the project.

Once they were laundered, she put tucks into the waistband of the knee breeches, moved the buttons over a little and patched the knees. The shirt was much too big. She nearly rebuilt it from scratch. She cut the arms off at the shoulders. It would be easier to shorten them there than at the cuffs. She took in the sides, cut several inches off the bottom and hemmed it, then sewed the sleeves back on. It was still too big, but she was no longer swimming in it.

When Ben came home that night, she greeted him with the costume on.

"I have to admit, it's not bad. If anyone looks closely they're likely to know you aren't a boy. But with luck they won't even notice you, much less look carefully."

"So, you'll take me?"

Ben nodded. "I still think it's a bad idea, but yes, I will."

Unfortunately, they woke the next morning to leaden skies and rain. As much as she wanted to go, slogging around all day in the rain wasn't enticing, so she agreed to wait until Friday.

Friday morning dawned clear and bright and Sara was beside herself with excitement.

As they sailed across the lagoon, Ben reissued all of the warnings he had given her since agreeing to the trip. "Stay in the area near San Marco. From the Arsenale, just walk along the water. If you get lost when you are in town, make your way west until you can see the cathedral tower or you reach water. From the water, you should be able to see the cathedral tower and work your way back to the square. Be careful. Avoid making eye contact with anyone. I'm going to give you a few *soldi* just in case you need it."

"You've already told me all of this, Ben."

"I know. I'm just praying that you listened and remember."

"I'll be fine. Stop worrying. What time shall I return to the Arsenale?"

"Don't return there. I'll move the boat closer to San Marco and meet you at the base of the tower. If anyone asks, your name is Sal. If they push, your parents are dead and you've just come here from Padua to live with an aunt. If they push more, she lives on Burano and makes lace."

"Why not just say she lives on the Lido? I'm at least familiar with that island."

"You may be, but you've never been to the village. Also, because so few people do live there, if the person questioning you knows anything at all about the Lido, they'll destroy that story in moments. More people live on Burano. It will be harder for them to disprove your story. But hopefully you can avoid any questions if you don't—"

"I know, if I don't make eye contact with anyone. Ben, I'll be fine."

So just after sunup, Sara found herself walking through Venice alone. San Marco square was quiet. She remembered reading about the Erbaria, a place near the Rialto Bridge where vendors set up stalls to sell fresh herbs, fruits, and vegetables.

She saw more people as she drew closer to the Grand Canal. But she had to stifle the odd giggle. Nearly all of these people were doing what in her time she'd have called the walk of shame. They all looked as if they'd been out all night and were just dragging home, still wearing their evening finery.

She crossed the Grand Canal at the Rialto Bridge and continued on to the Erbaria. She spent at least an hour wandering around the area, just soaking in the sights and smells, wanting to remember every detail. Once she'd absorbed her fill, she walked back to the Rialto until she found herself in the spot where, in her time, she had met Gertrude. It was absolutely mind-boggling that she had been here in this exact spot less than two weeks ago, two-hundred and forty-eight years from now.

She thought back to the events of that afternoon and realized that the little enclosed alley she had decided would act as her time portal was just down a little way on the other side of the canal. She had to see if it was there yet. Her whole story might be ruined if it wasn't. She crossed the bridge and began searching for the entrance. She didn't have the benefit of the little tourist gift shop with its stands full of postcards out front as her landmark. But eventually she did find it.

Oh. My. God. I can't believe it. She started to walk through it, then hesitated. What if it really was a time portal and she ended up in modern Venice again? She gave a little laugh. *Don't be silly. There is no such thing as a time portal.* She walked into the passage, but before she reached the opening onto the little square, the light at the end was blocked by a man entering it.

She kept going with her head down and avoiding eye contact as she'd promised Ben she would. But he stopped in front of her. Filling the small space.

"Well, what have we here?"

Sara wasn't sure what to say, so she said nothing, still keeping her head down.

"You're in my way, boy."

"Sorry, sir." She turned to go back the way she'd come, but he grabbed her arm, stopping her.

He grabbed her chin with his other hand, jerking her head upward. "I like pretty *boys* like you. Come with me. You can pay for blocking my way and if you are very good, I may find a *soldi* or two to give you."

What the hell had she been thinking when she accepted that watch? She'd done this for a romance novel and now was about to be molested. *You could have just used Google, Sara.* "N-n-no, sir," she stammered. "I—"

"Sal, lad, what's keeping ye?" came a familiar voice from behind the man.

The man let go of Sara. "You're really a boy? Go on to your granny." He pushed past Sara and continued down the passage.

Sara hurried toward the cloaked figure that stood in the little square. "Gertrude?"

"Of course. What are ye doing here? And dressed as a boy no less?"

"I have so much to tell you. I didn't drown."

The old woman cocked her head and grinned. "Evidently."

Sara laughed. "I mean, I was able to swim to the Lido. A man, Benedict MacIan, found me there and is letting me stay with him."

"I know all about Benedict MacIan. But that brings me back to my first question. Why are you here alone, dressed as a boy?"

"I told him about the watch and about how I want to learn all I can about eighteenth century Venice for my next book. He can only come with me on days when he isn't working and I don't have much time. I convinced him that this would be a way I could just sample life here."

Gertrude tsked and shook her head. "It doesn't surprise me that you'd think of that or that he wouldn't know why that's an awful idea. But you almost had a sample of life here that you wouldn't have liked. Come, we'll go have coffee and a bit of a chat."

"I only have a few *soldi*. I can't afford coffee. I thought Starbucks was pricey."

"I'll pay for our coffee. Caffè Florian won't be crowded this early in the morning."

"That's where I went with Ben. Maybe a café that's not right on San Marco Square will be more economical."

"Perhaps, but Florian's is the only café that allows women."

"You're kidding."

"I don't kid."

Sara fell in step beside Gertrude and they walked toward San Marco. As they passed a theatre called, Teatro San Luca, Sara paused and looked up at it. "This looks like the theatre that was right around the corner from my hotel in the twenty-first century."

"It is that theatre. It's called the Teatro Goldani now. As a matter of fact, Carlo Goldani is writing *Gl'innamorati*, The Lovers, not far from here, even as we speak."

Gertrude pointed out several sights as they walked, but didn't begin her "chat" until they were seated at Florian's and had been served. If the people at Florians disapproved of what appeared to be a street urchin in their midst, they didn't react.

"Ye needn't be worried about yer appearance, lass. When ye're with me, they only see and hear what I want them to see and hear. We can speak freely for now."

"How did you know...never mind."

Gertrude chuckled. "Learning, are ye? Good. So now back to the situation at hand. You are in *La Serenissima*, the Most Serene Republic of Venice, in the eighteenth century and there are a few things you need to know. This city is the most scandalous city in the world at the moment. It abounds with all sorts of vices. Political corruption, gambling, debauchery, and overall moral decay. Don't get me wrong, I'm not here to judge, but you must understand things to remain safe."

"Well, I knew courtesans were common, but…"

"My dear, courtesans are but one part of the entire culture. Frankly, the sexual revolution abounding in this city would rival that of the nineteen sixties in America. For example, many noblewomen have what they call a *cavalier servente*. A man with the same social standing as themselves who acts like a husband, at least a modern one. He dotes on her and escorts her to parties or the opera. And most of the time, he is her lover too."

"And their husbands are okay with this?"

"Their husbands are relieved by this. They have courtesans or perhaps are a *cavalier servente* to another noblewoman. You've written some historical romances. You know that noble marriages are arranged to form alliances, increase familial power and wealth, or any number of political reasons. Love is not part of the equation. Thus, all parties seek affection and romance outside of their marriage. It works for them."

"I see."

"As to courtesans, they are a uniquely liberated class of women. Many are highly educated, talented, poised, beautiful women who also are sexually adept and less restrained than noblewomen. And there are as many different kinds of courtesans as there are masculine appetites. Some men like lush, voluptuous curves, others older women with proven skills. Some men seek very slender women with boy-like figures. Thus, there are some courtesans who dress like boys. The man in that alley knew you were not a boy and assumed you were a courtesan or more likely, given the state of your attire, a prostitute."

Sara's mouth gaped in shock. "But that's why I dressed as a boy. Both Ben and I thought it would be safer."

"I can understand that. But Benedict has led a shockingly sheltered life for a man living in the Serene Republic. His parents were not Venetian and held different values. Because they lived apart, he wasn't exposed to some of the ordinary and perhaps seedier aspects of life here."

Sara sighed. "So, I can't spend time alone here. I'm limited to the seven Sundays I have left."

"What is it you want to see here, my dear?"

"Just an ordinary slice of life. I want to capture it as accurately as possible in my book."

Gertrude chuckled. "Little about Venice is ordinary. But if you want to experience what it is really like, maybe you need to meet someone better able to help you do that than Benedict. Perhaps a courtesan would be just the person."

"Really? Do you know someone who can introduce me?"

"My dear, I can introduce you. Shall we go now?"

"Yes, thank you. But don't we need to pay our bill?"

"It's already taken care of."

Once again, Sara followed Gertrude through the maze of Venice streets and alleys until she stopped in front of a door. "Here we are." She knocked.

A liveried servant came to the door. "Good morning. May I help you?"

Gertrude smiled. "Yes, thank you. Please tell *La Signora Peretti* that Gertrude is here to see her."

"Certainly. Allow me to show you into the drawing room."

"Thank you."

He led Sara and Gertrude into a well-appointed drawing room before delivering the message to his mistress.

They had barely taken their seats when they heard the clicking of rapid footsteps on the stairs and an amazingly

beautiful woman with olive skin, dark hair, and dark eyes
burst into the room.

"Gertrude! My favorite angel. I can't believe it's you.
It's been years."

Gertrude stood and opened her arms to hug the
woman. "Zina, my bonny lass, how are ye?"

"I'm well, thank you. I'd ask the same, but I know
you are supremely and perpetually well."

"Aye, that I am."

Zina's curious gaze swept over Sara. "And who is
this?"

"This is Miss Sara Wells. Sara, this is Rosina Peretti,
known to her friends as Zina."

"Lovely to meet you," said Sara, holding out her
hand.

Zina looked amused but accepted her handshake.
"Likewise. She's an American?" Zina asked Gertrude.

"Aye she is. But she accepted the pocket watch just a
little under two weeks ago, in this very city."

Zina grinned. "But in what year?"

"Before you did and that's all I'll say. 'Tis probably a
waste of precious time for the two of you to discuss the
future. So, let's get down to the important details. Sara is an
author of romance. She accepted the watch to gain in-depth

knowledge of Venice as it is now. She is staying with a friend on the Lido who isn't really able to show her much of the legendary side of Venice."

"Ah, you found her wandering around Venice looking like a delicious morsel?"

"Aye."

Zina turned to Sara. "That's a fantastic plot device, but it won't work here."

"So I learned. Gertrude rescued me."

"That's a very good thing." Zina turned her attention back to Gertrude. "So, you brought her to meet your favorite courtesan?"

Gertrude chuckled. "Something like that."

"Sara, do you want to pose as a courtesan?" Zina asked.

"No, I don't think I'd be able to pull that off."

"Hmm. Then perhaps the best way to do this is to have you act as a maid-servant to me. You will see plenty. I can give explanations when necessary and make sure you are safe. No one will bother you if you are with me."

Sara frowned. She didn't want to leave Benedict.

Gertrude smiled. "Zina, if I'm not much mistaken, Sara is enjoying the time she's spending with her new friend."

Zina grinned and arched an eyebrow. "I won't ask. It's better this way. But perhaps you would like to spend two or three days a week with me. You can pretend to teach me English. I've been pretending to learn for years, but no one has quite been successful." Zina laughed merrily. "So people freely speak English in front of me."

Gertrude shook her head in mock censure. "Honesty is a virtue, pet. Aim for it."

Zina laughed again. "Put away my wicked ways? Perhaps someday, Gertrude. What is it you say? Only time will tell."

"There's nothing wicked about ye, lass. The vast majority of wickedness lies in intent. You have a good heart and never forget that."

Zina smiled. "Thank you, Gertrude."

"Now, darlings, I am going to urge you to continue to not to exercise your natural curiosity concerning each other's pasts in the future. If you return, Sara, Zina will be somewhere in your time. It would be a tremendous temptation to find her, but you mustn't. And Zina, you might inadvertently say something that reveals some future event to Sara. That could have severe consequences. Live in the present."

Both women nodded.

Sara said, "I understand."

"I am desperately curious, but I'll hold my tongue," said Zina.

"Good. Well then, it's time for me to go." She opened her arms to Sara. "Give me a hug lass."

She stepped into the old woman's embrace and was immediately filled with the kind of warmth and confidence that she'd experienced the day she met Gertrude. "Thank you. Thank you for everything, Gertrude."

"You're very welcome." When she released Sara, she turned to Zina, "You too, lass. Give me a hug."

Zina melted into Gertrude's arms. "It's always so good to see you. Will you come again?"

"Only time will tell, lass. Only time will tell."

As Zina stepped out of the embrace, she swiped a tear from her cheek. "Well, I won't say goodbye anyway. Farewell."

"Farewell, lassies." And with that she vanished.

Sara looked at Zina. "Wait a minute, did you call her an angel?"

"Yes."

"So, she's an angel? A real angel?"

Zina shrugged. "She says she's called lots of things. None of them *encompass her true being*, but the word 'angel' works as well as any other."

Chapter 12

Benedict had been on edge all day, so the relief he felt when he saw her waiting for him by the tower was profound.

When she saw him, she practically skipped to him. "Ben, I have so much to tell you."

He wanted to wrap his arms around her and not let go, but he couldn't. "I can't wait to hear all about it, but perhaps you should wait until we are on our way."

She nodded. "That's probably best."

But the instant they were into the lagoon and out of earshot, she launched into her tale.

"Holy mother of God. A man accosted you? Even disguised as a boy? Thank God Gertrude was there to save you."

He shouldn't have been shocked by her explanation. He knew Venice had an underbelly that didn't match its outer beauty. "Well, that does it. You aren't going into Venice alone again."

"There's more to the story, Ben."

She went on to tell him about the courtesan named Zina who Gertrude introduced her to.

"She says the best way for me to get a real understanding of Venice is to spend some time with her."

"Gertrude thinks *that's* a good idea?"

"Yes. Zina suggested I pose as a servant or English tutor a few days a week."

Benedict frowned.

"I spent the day with her. Honestly, she knows so much about Venetian culture, I couldn't possibly find a better source for the information I need."

After much discussion, and once again against his better judgement, Benedict agreed that she could spend two days a week with Zina, the courtesan.

Sara wheedled three.

~ * ~

By Sunday night, Benedict was convinced he had entered one of the circles of hell. He'd nearly rather have the punishment the gods gave Sisyphus, perpetually rolling a boulder uphill only for it to roll back down. The frustration he felt being so near Sara, finding her so desirable on every level, and knowing she couldn't be his, might just kill him. Still, he'd rather have this time with her than none at all.

They didn't go into Venice that day. Since she would have the opportunity to spend so much time there over the next few weeks, she said she wanted to stay on the Lido and give him a taste of her culture.

"I want to take you on a picnic in the afternoon."

He wasn't sure what a picnic was, but he agreed and while he worked on Saturday, she prepared.

He went to Mass in the village. She would have liked to accompany him, but they both felt it better to keep her presence on the Lido as quiet as possible.

"I'll finish getting everything ready while you're gone," she promised. And true to her word, after he returned she was ready to go. She had a basket packed with fried chicken, tomato and cucumber salad, fresh bread and cherry crumble. On top of it all was a tablecloth and napkins. He wasn't sure where she thought the table would be, but he didn't comment.

She had another basket containing plates, utensils, cups, and three wine bottles.

"Don't you think that's a tad too much wine for one afternoon?"

"Only one of the bottles has wine in it. I filled one empty wine bottle with water and another with sweet tea."

"*Sweet tea?* I thought you took your tea black. Besides, it'll be cold in no time."

"I generally do drink hot tea black and the sweet tea is already cold. Since we don't have any ice, I chilled it in the well."

He frowned. "Why would you do that?"

"Because I like it. It's something we drink, especially in the summer. It is an absolute must for a picnic. We call it *iced* tea and if it's sweetened it's called sweet tea. Although strictly speaking, this isn't exactly sweet tea. Sweet tea is loaded with sugar. I like my tea just a little sweet."

Benedict had carried the baskets and Sara carried a linen sheet and some towels as they walked together to the edge of the sandy beach on the Adriatic side of the Lido. She spread the sheet in the shade under the trees, then arranged the tablecloth on the sheet and laid out their meal.

He'd had no clue what to expect from fried chicken, but it was delicious. The tomato and cucumber salad was cool and refreshing. Even the sweet tea wasn't bad. But the cherry crumble defied words.

When he couldn't eat another bite, he lay back with his hands under his head. "Sara, I think I like *picnics*. No, I love them. The meal was maybe the best I've ever eaten."

"Well, I was always told, 'the way to a man's heart is through is stomach.'"

"What?"

She laughed. "You know the old saying—no I guess you don't. The woman who first said that hasn't been born yet. But it means that if you feed a man well, he'll fall in love."

"Well it worked on me." *Christ, almighty, he'd said it. Just keep going and maybe she won't notice.* "Tell me about her."

She cocked her head to one side as if she hadn't quite worked out what he'd just said.

"I mean the woman who first said that."

"Oh. She was, or I guess will be, a newspaper columnist and author a hundred years from now. It was still really hard for women to be in the literary field then. She was a pioneer in many respects. She supported women's right to vote and she started the first club for women who were authors and artists."

"You really admire her."

Sara smiled. It was warm and wistful. Happy and sad at the same time. "I do admire her. My mother really admired her, too. She named me after her."

"What is her name?"

"She was published under the name Fanny Fern. But mom feared if she named me either one, kids would make fun of me. Those were really old fashioned names when I was born and the word 'fanny' had become slang for backside or even in some places, a woman's private parts."

He laughed and she smiled and blushed.

"Fanny Fern's real name was Sara Willis, so my parents named me Sara Fern Wells."

Sara fell silent and looked away, out towards the sea. A quiet melancholy slipped over her.

After a moment, Benedict sat up and reached for her hand. "I'm sorry."

Taking his hand, she smiled. "For what?"

"For reminding you of your loss."

"It's all right. I like remembering them, even if it makes me a little sad. My mom was a really strong woman and she wanted me to be one, too. She named me after a strong woman whom she admired. I think I wanted to be an author because of the things mom told me about Fanny Fern."

"You are a strong woman. I've never met anyone like you. If you are a product of your time, I think I would like it there."

She sighed. "I'd love to take you with me."

And there it was, the reminder that she was leaving. He needed to change the subject. "So tell me, Sara, what else do people do on picnics?"

She grinned. "Play games, or if they are at a beach like this, go swimming."

"Do you want to go swimming?"

"I'd love to go swimming, but I can't very well go in the water fully dressed."

"You could take off a few layers."

"No, that would be scandalous. What if someone saw me? I can't go swimming." But the look of yearning on her face told him she wanted to, whether it was scandalous or not.

"No one will see you. This beach is always deserted. I'll keep watch. If I see anyone in the distance, you can run back here and be dressed long before they're near enough to see."

She laughed. "You'd be near enough to see."

"Well, if it makes you feel any better, I've already seen you in a wet shift."

"I guess you have. And honestly, it covers more than my bathing suit at home does." She glanced back at the sea longingly. "Will you go with me?"

By all that was holy, would anyone say no to that? "Of course, I will."

Her face split into a grin. "All right. Let's do it."

He'd stripped down to only his breeches and she to her shift. Then he spent possibly the most delightful hour of his life swimming and playing in the water with her. His sea nymph, the girl from nowhere was back and he adored her. It was a blessing that the water was pleasantly cool. Otherwise, seeing her wet shift cling to her beautiful curves would have made him unpleasantly hard.

Now, hours later, he lay alone in his bed thinking of her and cursing himself for being a fool.

~ * ~

That afternoon was the first time Sara had seen Ben with his shirt off. When he walked across the sand in nothing but those tight-fitting breeches, she almost drooled. Then he waded into the sea, dove under the water, and surfaced again, pushing his wet hair back. The water on his pecs and washboard abs glistened in the sun. In her opinion, he was the epitome of male perfection, and she could happily stare at him all day.

But when he walked back towards the shallower water, his breeches having slipped low on his hips, something stirred her inside that wasn't remotely sisterly. Raw desire swept over her, taking her breath away. She imagined herself naked in his arms, in his bed—*no, Sara, channel this*. Kyra is the one who gets to jump his—that is Rafe's—sexy bones.

But as she lay in bed that night and sleep finally claimed her, it was not Kyra and Rafe she dreamed about.

Chapter 13

Sara's dreams did nothing to ease her carnal cravings. The next morning Ben took her across the lagoon in the gondola. Although Sara said she could walk from the Arsenale, Ben vetoed that.

"I will take you to Signora Peretti's house. You said it's on Rio de San Luca and that she has a *porta d'acqua,* a water door. I can take you directly there in the gondola and it will be much more discreet. If I'm seen sailing across the lagoon three days a week with the same woman, there will be talk. Furthermore, because Ceres's father is a merchant, he is well known among the owners of the shipyards. Someone could piece things together."

Inside the gondola's *felze*, she couldn't be easily seen.

But she could watch beautiful Ben as he rowed. *Stop this Sara. Put Kyra in this gondola and let her swoon over Rafe.*

When they arrived at the house, Ben helped her out and onto the steps of the water door, continuing to hold her hand for a moment. "I'll return for you between half-past five and six."

How could such casual contact be so seductive? Her mouth went dry. He'd said something to her.

"Is something wrong, Sara? Should I come later?"

Oh, right, the time he'll pick me up. "No, that'll be fine. I'll see you then."

He kissed her fingertips before stepping back and pushing away from the wall.

She watched him row away for a moment before knocking on the door.

The same manservant who had admitted them the previous day answered the door. "The signora is in her chamber. She asked that I send you up as soon as you arrived."

And so it started.

The first thing Zina did was clear up Sara's misconceptions about exactly what a courtesan was. Sara had thought of courtesans as…well, call-girls, high-priced prostitutes, but Zina explained that it wasn't quite that simple.

"Prostitutes walk the street or work in a brothel, most often because they have no choice. It's a last resort—sell themselves or starve. Courtesans choose the lifestyle and to be honest, sex is only a small part of it."

"The lifestyle?"

"Yes. Sara, in this time, unless you are born into the nobility, life is often drudgery. There are rules about what you are allowed to wear, what you are allowed to possess, and where you are allowed to go."

"Sumptuary laws?"

"Exactly. But those rules are ignored where courtesans are concerned. Frankly, there is little difference between a courtesan and a noblewoman except that a courtesan has much more freedom. In fact, it isn't uncommon for women of wealth who are widowed to become courtesans. There are even a few widowed noblewomen who see the benefits of our life."

"What are the benefits?"

Zina laughed. "A skilled courtesan is doted on by her noble benefactors. And what is her only responsibility? To be a beautiful and charming companion."

"What about the whole sex part? Doesn't that bother you?"

"Why should it? We are both from the twenty-first century. I knew loads of women there—all in serial monogamous relationships, mind you—who have slept with more men than I have. I enjoy sex and I know how to please a lover and ensure he pleases me. I see nothing wrong with that."

Sara had to agree with her. "I guess I understand that. I've only had a couple of boyfriends, but most of my friends in college had a good few. They'd say 'you have to kiss a lot of frogs before you find Prince Charming.' Still, maybe it's the romance writer in me, but I'd rather settle down with one man."

"And I can understand that. In fact, I did that. It was wonderful. I loved my husband with everything in me and I was equally adored."

"What happened?"

A shadow crossed Zina's face. "He died."

"Is that when Gertrude offered you the pocket watch?"

Zina shook her head. "She offered me the pocket watch *before* I was married. I met Alberto here. We fell in love and I stayed. We had a child." She paused for a moment, a sad smile on her face. "A perfect little boy who was the image of his father." She paused again, appearing to hold back tears. "Tragically, they both became ill at the same time and I lost them within days of each other. It was some sort of rapidly progressing respiratory infection and fever. That was fifteen years ago."

Fifteen years. "Oh, my God. Zina, I'm sorry."

"Thank you. It was a devastating loss."

"After it happened, did you regret staying?"

"No. Not for an instant. Roberto was the heart of my heart. I could never have left him."

Perhaps it was too intimate a question, but it had crossed Sara's lips before she could stop it. "Knowing what you know now, if you could have avoided all of the pain by not accepting the watch, would you have done that?"

"You mean choose never to know that kind of love? Simply to avoid the pain? No. It may be true that if you never say hello, neither will you have to say goodbye, but oh, my dear girl, what you would miss by doing so is almost unthinkable. Roberto was my soulmate. And never to have held my precious little Marco? No. The pain of their loss is a steep price to pay, but I have no regrets. Every moment with them was incomparably more valuable." She swiped a tear from her cheek. "I will see them again. I am confident of that. If I learned nothing else from the pocket watch it's that souls are real, unique, and exist beyond the mortal body. That's a great comfort."

"Did you leave a family behind? I mean parents and siblings and such."

Zina smiled. "Gertrude warned us not to go there, and now I think I know why. We could spend hours talking about our lives in the twenty-first century, but you have a limited amount of time and a lot to learn."

"You're right. What's first?"

"First, a courtesan must be beautiful." She laughed. "And as I get older, it takes longer and longer. Thankfully, the style in Venice is for a more natural look. In France and England, they use white makeup, which, if I remember correctly, contained lead and other heavy metals. Eww."

"You're exaggerating. It can't possibly take hours."

But it did. A hairdresser created an elaborate design every day, which never took less than an hour.

Over the next two weeks, Sara learned every detail of a courtesan's life. And she began to understand the appeal. Zina could go all over Venice, accompanied only by servants, and do largely whatever she wished. She had the wherewithal to buy jewels, books, lavish gowns, or coffee at Florian's. In fact, she went there most afternoons.

Sara looked terribly out of place. She was clean and comparatively well-dressed, but she clearly was neither a woman of society nor another courtesan. If they were rude enough to ask, Zina waived the question off with a laugh. "She's my new English tutor. We are practicing."

Sara loved coffee and, while tea was a reasonable substitute, she thoroughly enjoyed Florian's.

After one of these outings, they wandered through some side streets looking in shops. Sara stopped in front of a mask maker's shop, staring in awe at the beautiful creations.

"Lovely, aren't they," commented Zina. "It's a shame you won't be here for Carnivale. There is nothing like it on earth."

"Isn't it just like Mardi Gras?"

"Yes, but extended for six months."

"Six months?"

"It starts on the first Sunday in October, along with the new season of plays and operas. It stops for Advent and Christmas, then starts up again after Epiphany and goes on until the bells ring at midnight on Fat Tuesday. Even then, Venetians will use nearly any excuse to start it up again. For example, if a new Doge is elected, Carnivale starts."

"I would have liked to see it."

Zina's brows drew together.

"Is something the matter?"

"I was just thinking. It isn't exactly like Carnivale, but there is a masquerade ball on Saturday and I'm certain I can get an invitation for you."

"Really?"

"Absolutely. You will need a costume, but I'm bound to have something in my wardrobe that would be perfect for

166

you. Come here on Saturday instead of Friday and we can get you ready."

Sara hesitated to agree. It wasn't that she didn't want to go to the masquerade, she absolutely wanted to attend. But she didn't want to go without Ben.

"Is something the matter, dear?"

"Um. Well, I was wondering...I mean, I hate to ask but do you think it would be possible for me to bring...uh...a friend?"

A slow smile spread across Zina's face. "A *friend*? The friend Gertrude said you were living with? Sara, are you living with *a man*?"

"Yes, but just platonically." Sara blushed profusely, mostly because while she and Ben hadn't done anything, the sexual tension she felt was overwhelming.

Zina chuckled. "Well, that is a shame. But, yes, your invitation will be for you and an escort. I would have arranged one for you if you didn't so conveniently have a *friend* who can serve that function."

Sara squealed like a schoolgirl. "I can't believe it, I'm going to a Venice masquerade ball."

~ * ~

Benedict could hardly believe his ears. "No, Sara. I'm sorry but we are not attending a society ball."

"Ben, please. It's a masquerade ball in Venice. Even in my time, Venice is still known for its masks and lavish masquerade balls. I can't pass up an opportunity like this."

"You don't understand, sweetling. Something like this is way beyond my social circle."

"What do you mean? You are a successful businessman."

"Yes I am, but even if I'm prosperous, I am firmly a member of the bourgeoisie. My father came to Venice as a poor Scottish carpenter. People like me aren't invited to those kinds of events."

"But we will be invited. Zina is taking care of it."

"Sara, I don't think…what if someone recognizes you?"

"Masquerade, remember? Come on, we've got to do this. How can we pass it up?"

He looked into her blue eyes and saw how much she wanted to go to the ball. How could he deny her this simple request? *Because it isn't so simple and it might be dangerous*, said an inner voice.

"Please, Ben."

The longing in her eyes broke his resolve. "Okay, I will take you the masquerade on Saturday, but you must agree to leave with me immediately if I ask you to."

"Deal."

Chapter 14

Benedict wasn't surprised to find Sara already up when he woke on Saturday. She had breakfast nearly on the table when he arrived downstairs. "Sara, please tell me you haven't been up for hours. You will be exhausted by the time the masquerade ball starts if you have been."

She laughed. It was a sound he couldn't get enough of.

"No, I haven't been up long. I'm just really excited. Never in my wildest dreams did I imagine this would be possible. What would a book set in historic Venice be if it didn't have at least one masked ball?"

"What indeed?" One more reminder that she was leaving wasn't what he wanted this morning. He wanted to savor her excitement and find himself caught up in it.

"Thank you again for escorting me. I know you think you'll be uncomfortable, but I've had an idea."

He smiled. "What's your idea?"

"It's a masquerade. No one there will know us. Even if there are a few people there who might know you, as you pointed out last night, they would never expect to see you there. Furthermore, they won't recognize you with a mask."

"That's probably true."

"So we can be anyone we want to be and no one will know the difference. You be the eldest son of an extremely affluent merchant who has become disillusioned by those seeking a marriage contract with you solely because of your wealth. You are pretending to be ordinary. Maybe a clerk in an office."

Humoring her he said. "Fine. I'm a rich man pretending to be average instead of the average man that I am pretending to be rich."

"You aren't average, Ben, but I'll ignore that statement for a while. I'll be the daughter of an impoverished nobleman who seeks to marry me to a man of means who can dig us out of debt. So far, he has proposed one old rich man after another, none of whom are acceptable to me. He has grown impatient now and has given me the choice of three men. I am to make my decision tonight. I reluctantly agree, but before I'm introduced to the first of his choices, I meet a young clerk who steals my heart. He, of course, believes he has found a girl who isn't trying to marry him for his money."

"I see where this is going."

"Good, we'll get there faster. You spend the evening avoiding detection from your admirers and I spend the evening avoiding my father."

He chuckled. "It sounds like a potential disaster."

She grinned. "Oh, it could be. But it's equally possible that they fall in love, decide to get married, and run away together."

"Is this going in your book?"

"Of course, it is. But it will be fun, don't you think? More fun than worrying about what other people think of us."

"Then I'll do it. For you and for the benefit of your readers." And maybe, for a little while, he would be able to pretend that she'd be his forever.

Her face lit in the bright happy smile that made her even more beautiful than she already was. "It's a plan then. Are you ready to go?"

"I am."

"Aren't you bringing your dress clothes to change into?"

"I don't think it's necessary. I am not going to work the entire day. I'll come back over here in the early afternoon, so I can wash and shave before dressing. I'll meet you at Zina's house at the appointed hour."

~ * ~

By midmorning Benedict realized that he was much more excited about attending the ball with Sara tonight than he liked to admit. He was completely unable to focus, so he left the shipyard earlier than he had planned. He made a slight detour on his way home to purchase a mask.

He found it no easier to be at home with time on his hands. The silence pressed in on him. He had lived in this house, alone, for years. It had never bothered him before. But over the last three weeks, he hadn't spent a single moment here alone. He wasn't sure how he'd manage after she left.

Finally, the hours ticked by and it was time to go. Bathed, shaved, and dressed in his finest suit, he examined himself in the looking glass. He smiled when he remembered the charade that Sara had suggested that morning. He looked slightly better dressed than the young clerk he would pretend to be, but not as flashy as many men of his standing might. "You'll do."

He rowed the gondola across the lagoon and past the Doge's palace, until he reached Rio di San Moisè, which led ultimately to Rio de San Luca, and Zina's home.

A liveried servant admitted him, showed him to the receiving room, offered him a glass of wine, and informed him that the signora and Miss Wells would be down shortly.

"Shortly" might have been a bit of an overstatement. It had to have been well over a quarter of an hour and they still hadn't joined him. To keep from pacing, he had positioned himself by a window that looked out on the canal and counted the gondolas that passed.

Finally, the door opened behind him. He turned towards it and froze. Sara had just stepped into the room and she was stunning. She wore a breathtaking gown of white and pale gold brocade, cut low enough to reveal the top curve of her breasts. Panniers extended the width of the skirt on both sides. Her black curls had been piled on her head in an intricate arrangement and then powdered. She wore very little make-up, perhaps a touch of color on her lips and cheeks. It pleased him that she didn't wear one of the little black patches women often wore to conceal a scar or blemish or simply to appear coquettish.

From behind Sara, an equally beautifully dressed woman who appeared to be in her mid to late thirties said, "It looks like *your friend* approves." This could only be Zina Peretti.

"I certainly do. Sara, you are exquisite." Benedict made a small bow. "Good evening, Signora. I'm Benedict MacIan."

"Yes, Sara has told me a bit about you. She's very grateful for the help you have given her."

"It's been my pleasure."

A slow smile spread across her face. "I'm sure it has."

Benedict didn't quite know what to say to that.

Zina gave a tinkling laugh at his discomfiture. "Well, my darlings, I think you should go to the ball in my gondola tonight. As handsome a figure as I'm sure you cut wielding an oar, Mr. MacIan, perhaps you'd like to ride with this *exquisite* creature tonight."

"Aren't you going with us?" asked Sara.

"I'll see you there, but I'll be going with one of my benefactors. He'll be calling for me here any minute."

"Thank you for everything, Zina. I feel like Cinderella."

"Well, here's a bit of advice from your ersatz fairy godmother." She lowered her voice as if revealing a state secret. "Don't let Prince Charming out of your sight. He might be eaten alive."

Sara laughed.

"I'm not kidding," said Zina.

~ * ~

Nothing to Lose

Sara hadn't quite believed the reflection that stared out at her from Zina's floor length looking glass. She had never worn anything more stunning in her life. But the awestruck way Ben looked at her made her feel beautiful.

He helped her into Zina's gondola. It was larger than Ben's and the *felze* was more lavishly appointed. When he was seated beside her, the gondolier pushed off, heading toward the Grand Canal.

"Your beauty overwhelmed me so, I didn't even ask the Signora where this ball is being held."

"You clean up pretty well yourself. And I guess I was more focused on the fact that I was going to a masquerade ball than where it would be. I suppose the gondolier must know."

"Let's hope so. Otherwise we could float around the canals of Venice all evening." He grinned. "But now that I've said it, I'm not sure that would be a bad thing."

They chatted about inconsequential things and donned their masks as they floated down the Grand Canal. Ben helped tie the ribbons of her gold filigree mask and adjusted the three ostrich feathers affixed to one side so they arched jauntily over her hair.

In turn, she helped tie his mask on. He had opted for a relatively plain black mask instead of the long-nosed mask preferred by most Venetian men. She laughed when he explained, "It's hard to whisper in a beautiful woman's ear with a nose like that getting in the way."

It seemed like it had been only minutes since they left Zina's home when the gondolier maneuvered next to a building.

Ben glanced out the window and stiffened. "The ball is at Palazzo Balbi?"

Sara frowned. "Is something wrong with that?"

"No. I mean…well I don't know. Palazzo Balbi is owned by Joseph Smith, the British Consul to Venice."

"Is that a problem?"

"It's just that Reese Llewellyn is a very wealthy British merchant. It is extremely likely that he'll been in attendance tonight."

Sara felt the color drain from her face. "We shouldn't go. We'll ask the gondolier to take us back."

Ben caressed her cheek. "Sara, we don't have to go in. But this is something that you really wanted to do. I don't want you to regret not taking the opportunity. You are dressed in Venetian-made finery befitting a noblewoman. Your hair is powdered and you will be wearing a mask. I suspect you could come nose to nose with Llewellyn and he wouldn't recognize you. But the decision is yours."

Sara took a deep breath. Ben was right. This might be her only opportunity to ever attend a ball like this one, she wouldn't squander it. Resolved she said, "Let's go."

Ben nodded decisively and helped her out of the gondola. When they entered the palazzo, he glanced casually around before leaning next to her ear and whispering, "He doesn't seem to be here. At least not yet."

As guests arrived, they were ushered into the receiving line to be presented to their host and hostess, Consul Smith and his wife, Elizabeth Murray. It was slightly unsettling, and as was her nature, Sara began to fidget. As she looked around nervously, she realized Zina had been right, several women were eyeing Benedict and attempting to garner his attention.

Ben took her right hand in his and placed his left hand on the small of her back. His casual touch served to calm her jangled nerves.

"You are causing a stir," she whispered to him.

"It isn't me they're staring at. It's you."

She had to stifle a laugh. "I'm pretty sure it's not me. Maybe they think Casanova is hiding under that mask."

He shook his head. "Not a chance. He's being held in the prison at the Doge's palace."

"Really?" Sara knew Casanova was a public figure in the eighteenth century and that he had lived at least part of his life in Venice, but she wasn't sure of when that was exactly. "Why is he in prison?"

Ben chuckled. "I believe he was charged with *an affront to religion and common decency.* But tell me, lovely Sara, how is it you know about Giacomo Casanova?"

"Let's just say his reputation made the history books…and romance novels."

"Indeed? I would not have imagined that."

They had finally reached the front of the line and were presented as Mr. Benedict MacIan and Miss Sara Wells. Pleasantries were exchanged briefly before they were absorbed into the crowd at the ball.

They found a spot near a window from which they could watch the dancers. Somehow, Sara had always found the idea of formal court dances very romantic. They were precise ceremonious dances that were meant to mirror the proper, restrained courtship procedures of the day. Presented with them now, she found them dull.

Ben said, "I'm sorry, I've never really learned to dance."

"Don't worry, unless they start a country-western line dance, I can't join in either. And honestly, I think watching paint dry might be more engaging."

He laughed. "Then we must find other entertainment."

And at that moment, the magic began.

He leaned closer to her ear and whispered "My lady, I don't believe we've been introduced."

She frowned. "Excuse me?"

"I said, I don't think we've been introduced. My name is Ben and I am definitely *not* the disillusioned eldest son of an extremely affluent merchant. I'm just an ordinary man. I work as a humble clerk to *Signore Maximus Importanti*."

She grinned broadly. He was playing the game she'd proposed. "*Signore Maximus Importanti?*"

"Yes. And while he is a very important man, I am not."

"Well then, I'm pleased to make your acquaintance." She curtsied. "My name is Sara *Senza Soldi*, and frankly I'm just trying to avoid my father, *il Duca Senza Soldi*."

He laughed richly. "Really? The Duke of No Money?"

In all seriousness she answered, "Yes, have you met him?"

Ben made a valiant attempt to stop laughing. "No, I don't suppose I have. But, why, dear lady, are you trying to avoid your father?"

"Because he is seeking a betrothal for me."

"You are certainly of an age to marry. Why do you wish to avoid it?"

"He has given me an ultimatum. I must decide between one of three men tonight. But I can't."

"You can't decide? Perhaps I may offer you some assistance. Describe for me the best quality of each of your suitors."

"No, you misunderstand me. I don't *want* to marry any of them."

"Still, if you must, perhaps together we can discern who the best candidate is."

She gave a melodramatic sigh. "I suppose it must be done."

"Clearly. So, enumerate their best qualities for me, please."

Sara thought for a moment. "Hmmm. This is difficult. Where to start? Tell me, *Signore*, how do you believe great wisdom is attained?"

Ben shrugged. "I would say wisdom comes with age. It is a product of experience."

"Well then, I suppose the best thing that can be said for *Signore Antico*—"

"Mr. Old?"

"Yes, *Signore Antico*. His best quality is that he has had many opportunities to gain wisdom. Many, many, many, many opportunities. His dear friend, *Signore* Methuselah, can attest to that."

Ben laughed again.

She continued. "And then there is…uh…*Signore Parsimonioso*."

"Mr. Thrifty?"

She nodded. "Yes. He has amassed a great fortune."

"There are worse things than being married to a rich man."

"I suppose so…"

"Tell me, Sara, how has *Signore Parsimonioso* managed to build such wealth. Are his gains from dishonest sources?" He folded his arms on his chest.

She shook her head. "Oh, no. His riches come from a perfectly legal, time honored, proven method."

Ben nodded sagely. "I see, so he inherited it."

Sara laughed outright. "Indeed, and has never spent a single *soldo* on anyone but himself. For example, one evening we were dining together and he selected a bottle of wine—an excellent vintage. He poured a drop of water into his own glass before filling it with wine."

"There's nothing wrong with that. Some people believe a drop of water brings out some of the more subtle flavors in a glass of fine wine."

"Perhaps, but then he poured a drop of wine into my glass before filling it with water."

It looked as if Ben was struggling not to laugh. "Hmm. I can see how that might be a problem. What about the third man?"

"That would be *Signore Idiota.*"

"Oh dear. That doesn't sound promising. I hesitate to ask but, what is his best quality?"

She smiled. "He's very funny. He makes me laugh."

"A sense of humor is a wonderful thing. Maybe he is the man for you."

"No. You see, I don't think he actually intends to be funny, but it's hard not to laugh at the things he does."

"Give me an example."

She grinned. This was going to be fun. All she had to do was recycle Daphne jokes. "Well, about three months ago someone told him that most accidents occur at home."

"So, what did he do?"

"What could he do? He moved."

Ben chuckled.

"Then there's the time I told him that we probably shouldn't be married because I'm a year older than he is. He said, 'that isn't a problem, we can wait until next year.'"

Ben chuckled again. "I see what you mean."

"There is one good thing though."

"What's that?"

"If I need a break from him, I just give him a piece of paper with 'turn the page over' written on both sides. It occupies him for hours."

Ben guffawed.

This was fun. Sara imagined a similar scene in her book. One in which Rafe laughed and teased with Kyra. That was the kind of scene she found most romantic, and loved to write, but had never actually experienced. *You're experiencing it now*, said a little voice within her.

They continued to play the game for perhaps three quarters of an hour, Ben asking questions and Sara painting an absolutely dreadful picture of her three fictitious suitors.

Ben ruled out *Signore Parsimonioso* almost immediately. "He loves his money first and best, so it is the mistress he loves best. It's highly unlikely he'll squander it away gambling or pour it lavishly on a courtesan. But he will guard it jealously from you as well. You will live like a pauper and that would be tragic."

Next Ben considered *Signore Idiota*. "He may be a fool, but there could be advantages to that. For if you marry him, by necessity you will have complete control over the household for to put him in charge of anything more challenging that dressing himself would be imprudent. Not to mention that having laughter in one's life is a very good thing."

Yes, a very good thing indeed. Sara nodded. "I see your points, but I fear for the children we would have. Because in my experience when a man is a fool, more often than not, his son is a bigger fool. No, I think *Signore Antico* is the one I must choose."

"Are you sure?" asked Ben. "Being married to a man that old is likely to be pure misery."

"I'm certain it will be. But on the bright side, it won't be for long. He's already got one foot in the grave and the other one is slipping."

He laughed. "Nevertheless, it would be a crime to marry you to the old geezer for even a day. Maybe we should see if your father would consider a fourth suitor."

"Pray tell, who?"

He cocked his head to one side. "Me."

Yes, please. How wonderful would it be to be married to him? But she couldn't. She had to go back, didn't she? She tried to push the thought of marrying Ben out of her mind. *Focus on the novel, that's why you're here.* This scene would be an absolutely perfect point in the book for Rafe to kiss Kyra for the first time.

As if he had read her mind, Ben slipped one hand behind her neck and, caressing her cheek with the other, he kissed her softly, then nipped at her lower lip.

She opened her mouth to him.

Ben emitted a soft groan, pulled her closer, and deepened the kiss.

She melted into him. Ben's kiss was warm and soft, yet demanding. The ballroom became a dim blur of sound and color, too far away to matter. The only real things in her world were his arms around her and his lips on hers. She had longed to be in Ben's arms and for him to kiss her. Truthfully, she had longed for a kiss like this her whole life.

And in that moment Sara knew she'd been fooling herself. This trip to the past, this *soul exchange*, was never meant to be about a romance novel. Her soul had travelled through time because this is where her soulmate was.

When their lips parted, Ben rested his forehead against hers. "Sara. I have tried. I swear to you I have, but I'm failing miserably."

"What are you talking about?"

"Sweetling, I love you. I can't bear to lose you. I have no right to ask and I will understand if you say no—"

She took his face in her hands, stood on tiptoe and silenced him with a kiss before saying, "Ben, I love you. I don't want to leave you. Ever."

"You'll stay?" The note of wonderment in his voice pulled at her heart.

"I'll stay."

"Oh, thank God. I adore you and I'm certain if you left, you'd take my heart with you forever. He gave her another quick kiss. "So, there is something I must ask you. Sara Fern Wells, my precious girl, will you marry me?"

Her hand fluttered to her mouth and tears welled in her eyes. "Yes, Ben, I love you with all my heart and I'll marry you."

He leaned down to kiss her again, just as movement across the room caught her eye. When she realized it was Zina making her way through the crowd on the arm of a large man wearing a mask and powdered wig, Sara went rigid. There was no part of him that she could see, but she knew instantly he was Ceres's father.

"We have to leave. Now." She hissed. She looped her arm through his and headed in the opposite direction.

"What's wrong?"

"Zina was walking towards us with a man. Based on the fear I'm feeling, I think it's Llewellyn."

Ben didn't pause to look. He maneuvered them through the festive crowd until they reached the stairway that led to the reception room. Just before they ducked out of the room, he glanced back.

"You're right. I think it's him and Zina is trying to get your attention. We need to leave, and if we go by gondola they will catch up to us on the dock." When they reached the level of the receiving room, instead of heading to the water door, he led her out a door on the opposite side. They hurried down a hall that went through to the back of the building.

Once outside he clasped her hand and turned to the right, nearly running to the end of the alley. He paused, glanced both ways, and made a small jog to the left before entering another alley that ended at a small bridge over a canal. They crossed the bridge and turned right.

She had a death grip on his hand as, for the next ten minutes, he wound his way through the narrow streets, crossed two more canals until they reached a piazza in front of a church.

He stopped for a moment. "I think we can take a moment to catch our breath."

"Where are we?"

He looked up at the church. "That's the church of Saint Apollonia."

"Where are we going?"

He smiled. "We are going back to Zina's to get the gondola. Just down this alley and to the right is the church of San Silvestro. There is a *traghetto pier* there."

"What's a *traghetto*?"

"It's sort of a ferry across the Grand Canal. Do they not have them in the future?"

"They might. I'm not sure. There are four bridges across the canal now instead of just one."

"Once we cross, it will just take a few minutes to walk to Zina's house."

"What if Ceres's father is already there with her?"

"I doubt they will be. They may not even have followed us down the stairs. It looked like she was just trying to get your attention. But even so, it won't matter. The gondola is moored close to the alley by her house. I'll be able to reach it from there, without entering the house."

He had been right. When they reached San Silvestro, they didn't have to wait long for the *traghetto* and they reached Zina's house a few minutes later.

Sara finally breathed a sigh of relief when Ben piloted the gondola out of *Rio di San Moisè* into the east end of the Grand Canal and were headed for home across the lagoon.

Chapter 15

Sara had agreed to marry him. As he rowed across the lagoon, he allowed that to sink in. He couldn't have wiped the happy smile off his face if his life depended on it.

Even so, their rapid departure from the ball was unsettling. While weaving their way through the streets of Venice, he'd wondered if this flight was completely necessary. He was going to marry her. They'd have to face Ceres's father at some point. But Sara's fear in the moment had been intense. And because she couldn't explain it, he thought it prudent to act on it and sort out Llewellyn later.

After he tied the gondola to his little dock, he helped Sara out of the *felze*. He smiled. She had used the time while they crossed to remove the pins and shake some of the powder from her hair. Her curls hung around her shoulders, her gown coated with more powder than her hair now.

When she stood on the dock beside him, alone under the moonlight, he kissed her again. More languorously this time. After all, a lifetime lay ahead of them. He wasn't quite sure how long they stood there, locked in an embrace.

When he ended the kiss, she took his hand and stepped away. "Shall we go home now?"

Home. "Yes, my love, let's go home."

They walked silently up to the house, her hand in his. Perhaps his grip was a little strong, but she held on equally as tightly. It was almost as if, having just realized they were meant to be together, they didn't want to risk losing one another.

Once they entered the house, Benedict took her face in his hands and kissed her again, more heatedly than before. Her arms slid around his neck and she returned his ardor. He practically forced himself to end the kiss and pull slightly away. "My darling girl, I love you and I want to make you mine, but we aren't married yet. I know things are different in your time, but wouldn't dishonor you for anything."

Sara shook her head. "There is no dishonor in the expression of love and I do love you. We will be married soon. I want to make love with you." She took his hands in hers and smiling coyly, stepped back towards the stairs, pulling him with her. "Come upstairs with me."

Benedict groaned, wanting nothing more. "You're certain?"

"Absolutely certain."

"Aye, then, I'll go upstairs with you."

She turned and still holding on to one of his hands, lifted her skirts with the other, and practically ran up the stairs. When they reached his bedroom, he covered her lips with his own, kissing her deeply again.

She responded. This time, instead of encircling his neck with her arms, she started working at the buttons on his waistcoat, then his shirt. Pulling it from his breeches, she put her hands under the fabric and stroked his chest with her small, soft hands.

He broke the kiss long enough to pull the shirt over his head. Her hands continued to roam over his body as he returned the favor, pulling at laces and buttons to free her from the beautiful brocade dress. "Women wear too many clothes," he murmured as he tried to untie the panniers.

"I couldn't agree more," she said, stopping her exploration of his body to rid herself of several pesky layers even as he undid the many buttons on his breeches.

Finally, they were both free of their garments. She stood before him, the moonlight through the window casting a magical glow around her.

"You are magnificent, Sara, and you take my breath away."

"I could say the same about you." She stepped toward him, her naked body molding against his. "But I'm not in the mood to talk." She stood on tiptoe pressing her lips against his. "Make love to me, Ben," she whispered.

"I can deny you nothing, my beautiful girl." He lifted her in his arms and crossed the room to lay her gently on the bed before lying down beside her.

Her small hands roamed over his chest and shoulders. Although tentative and feather-light at first, her touch enflamed his passion. She slipped her hands down his sides and across his belly, brushing the crisp hair that led to his groin. He moaned and grabbed her hands. "Ah, Sara, my love, I can't bear it."

She smiled. "You said you could deny me nothing."

He chuckled. "I also said I'd make love to you, but I've wanted you for so long, if you torture me so, I won't be able to keep that promise."

He pulled her hands to his lips and kissed them. Then still holding her hands in his, he moved them over her head and captured her lips in another kiss, before trailing kisses down the slender column of her throat. With aching slowness, he eventually reached his goal, her round creamy breasts. He enclosed one pert nipple in his mouth and suckled, gently teasing with his tongue. He released her hands, cupping the other breast, massaging it lightly before sliding his hand over her silky belly to the dark curls at the apex of her legs.

She arched into his touch, almost purring with delight.

He put the heel of one hand over her most private part, massaging with a circling motion, gently increasing the pressure.

Her hands went to his shoulders, clinging to him and lifting her hips to increase the pressure even more.

If she needed more, he'd give her more, and he slipped his thumb inside to circle the sensitive spot, pleased when she writhed against his touch. As her pleasure built, he slipped a finger inside. He slowed his movements slightly for a moment, watching her.

"You are so beautiful, Sara."

Lost in pleasure, she simply moaned and arched against his hand. He positioned himself over her, continuing to rub and tease with his hands. When she panted, arching her head back and beginning to tremble with her release, he slid his hardness into her with one firm thrust. He felt her muscles continue to contract, even as she gave a small cry. As much as he craved his own release, he held very still within her, watching as the tremors of her climax swept through her.

~ * ~

Nothing to Lose

Sara was not a virgin, but Ceres was. Still, she'd never had a lover who focused so completely on her. When Benedict entered her at the peak of her release, she cried out, but it wasn't from pain. It was from the sheer bliss of joining so completely with him. Any discomfort became so melded with the waves of bliss coursing through her, she didn't care.

She took his face in her hands and pulled him to her lips. She kissed him with abandon, threading her fingers through his hair and holding him to her. But he held rigidly still. "Sweetheart, you can move."

"I've hurt you. I don't want to make it worse."

"But you haven't hurt me. Please, let me give you what you crave."

He groaned but began to move very slowly. As he moved, she felt the heat growing in her belly once more. She moved with him, rising to meet him, pushing him to move faster. A driving need coursed through her until once again, she trembled as waves of ecstasy swept through her body yet again. And as her muscles contracted around the hard length of him, he cried out and she felt the warm rush of his seed within her. "Dear God, Sara…" His voice trailed off. He panted and lowered his forehead to hers.

"That was spectacular," she finished his sentence.

He chuckled and kissed her. "Absolutely spectacular."

He withdrew from her, and laid on his side next to her, pulling her against him.

"Mmm. I love spooning," she said.

"Spooning?"

"We are nestled like spoons in a drawer. Where I come from we call it spooning."

"Spooning. Yes, I think I quite like it, too."

That was the last thing she remembered as she drifted off to sleep.

Chapter 16

Most of Sunday was spent in each other's arms. Sara had never felt like this before. Benedict completed her. The modern woman in her was briefly appalled by that sentiment. Still, it was the right word. It wasn't as if she had been missing or searching for something. No, she had been a complete person before. But there was something different now. They had become one, two parts of something greater than each had been alone. She had certainly never felt this about any other man—even those few who she thought she had loved.

This must be what it felt like to find one's soulmate.

When Monday morning came, neither of them were ready to re-enter the real world, but there was work to be done and a marriage to arrange.

After breakfast, Sara said, "I'll just go get the ball gown Zina loaned me and I'll be ready to go."

"Go?"

"Yes, I need to go to Zina's."

"But, sweetling, if you are staying, there is no reason to pretend to be a maidservant any longer. I can return the dress for you."

"It isn't just the dress, Ben. We fled that party without a word to anyone. I owe her an explanation."

He nodded. "I suppose you do. Shall I speak to her with you? What if Llewellyn is there?"

"One of the servants will answer the door. If Zina is occupied, we will leave. But if she isn't, I think it might be better for me to see her alone first. Besides, weren't you going to find out what we need to do to be legally married?"

"Yes, I was. The sooner that is accomplished, the happier I'll be."

When they arrived at Zina's house, the servant who answered the door confirmed that the *Signora* was alone and expecting her.

Ben handed the ball gown and all of its accoutrement to her.

"Thank you." Sara gave him a quick kiss. "Will you return at the usual time?"

"No. I only intend to go to the shipyard briefly this morning. Then I'll sort out the marriage details. I'll return for you at midday."

She smiled broadly. "Good. I'll see you then."

She observed him push off the wall and begin rowing down the canal before she entered the house. She was certain she'd never tire of watching him.

The servant took the garments from her before she practically ran up to steps to Zina's rooms.

Of course, Zina hadn't dressed for the day yet. She wore a dressing gown as she lounged on a chaise, sipping hot chocolate. "Well, well, well. You have a bit of explaining to do. I'm certain you saw me before dashing the other direction in a manner befitting Cinderella. I half expected to find that you'd left a slipper behind."

The twinkle in Zina's eyes suggested that she was more curious than offended.

"I'm sorry, Zina. It was terribly rude of me, but I can explain."

"Then explain away. Sit down. Pour yourself a cup of chocolate first if you wish."

Sara took the chair across from Zina. "No, thank you. Perhaps when I've finished the story."

"Suit yourself, but don't make me wait any longer."

"Well, I guess the most exciting bit is that we realized how much we loved each other. I decided to stay and he's asked me to marry him."

A slow smile spread across Zina's face. "Two more misplaced soulmates brought together. I wondered if that might happen. When I saw the way he looked at you, I knew he had fallen hopelessly. But you were all caught up in thinking this was research for your book."

Sara chuckled. "You're right. I wouldn't let myself think of anything else. As soon as I got here, I worried that I might get caught up in the romance of it all and make a bad decision. I had a boyfriend in the twenty-first century and I really thought I loved him. But what I feel for Ben isn't even remotely the same as my feelings for Mark. Last night I finally admitted it to myself."

"Excellent. But why didn't you just rush across the ballroom to gush this wonderful news to me when it happened?"

"Because of the man you were with. Tell me, is he one of your benefactors?"

"When he's in Venice, yes. He's a merchant and travels quite a bit. But why would that have stopped you."

Sara took in a deep breath, letting it out slowly. "Um…when Gertrude gave you the watch, did she tell you about the possibility that some of the other person's memories would leak through?"

"Yes. I have experienced it from time to time."

"Well, so have I. From the instant I arrived, I felt her fear. I didn't know who she was and I wasn't quite sure what she was afraid of, but I had the sense that I should be hiding."

"What do you mean, you didn't know who she was? I thought she was a friend of Benedict's."

"No. He found me. You see, when my soul entered this body, I was in the sea, my heavy clothes becoming wet and pulling me under."

A look of horror crossed Zina's face.

"I was able to get them off and swim to the Lido, but I was exhausted and collapsed. Benedict found me the next morning."

"Oh, dear God. You are Ceres Llewellyn."

Sara nodded. "I think so. About a week after he found me, Ben heard about Llewellyn's daughter having fallen overboard."

"Why didn't you tell the poor man? He has been sick with worry."

"Ben wanted to, but I talked him out of it. I have felt a deep sense of fear, of needing to get away from something or someone and I'm fairly certain it's Ceres's father. But I also fully believed that I would be returning to my own time at the end of sixty days. It seemed cruel to let him think his daughter had been found, only to have her die within two months. Since Ceres would have died as a result of falling or jumping overboard, it seemed best to let everyone who knew her think she had."

Zina shook her head slowly. "I understand. I guess in the same circumstances I might have done the same thing. But now you aren't leaving."

"I know, but I can't get over the sense of foreboding. Do you know why Ceres might be afraid of her father?"

"Let me tell you a bit about Reese Llewellyn. He has been a benefactor of mine for several years. He is smart, handsome, and exceedingly wealthy. He treats me like a princess, but he is very demanding and expects to be obeyed. When he is in town, I see no one else."

Sara frowned.

"Don't get me wrong. He isn't abusive, just authoritative."

"Then why is Ceres afraid?"

"Over the years, Reese has shared very little about his private life. I only know a few bits of information about his wife. I believe he loved her deeply. I suspect she had a significant dowry that helped him build his business to what it is today. And she died giving birth to their daughter. I know a bit more about Ceres. He doted on her and talked about her a lot. She had the best of everything, including a bevy of tutors. As far as I can tell, she was given an education that most men would envy. Perhaps that's why she longed to go on the Grand Tour."

"Do women do that?"

"A few. Reese refused to allow it, but she was relentless. I don't suppose it helps that until then, he had given her every little thing she desired. 'No' was a foreign concept. But she did scale back her request. She didn't care about visiting Paris or Florence or any of the other major stops on the Grand Tour. All she really wanted was to come here to Venice."

"Why?"

"Apparently, she was a rather talented artist and this would have been one of the finest places in the world for her to study. He still wouldn't allow it. Part of me thinks that to have his daughter here would bring his two separate worlds together and he didn't want that."

"So she ran away to Venice with a maid. Benedict had learned that much."

"Yes, she posed as a widow, wore all black, covered herself with heavy veils and simply booked passage on a ship. No one questioned her. She brought a maid and a sizable chunk of money with her. When he returned home and found her missing, he was furious. He boarded his fastest ship and even though it didn't have its complete cargo yet, he left for Venice immediately. He was several days behind her, still his ship managed to catch up to hers just off shore. According to her maid, she believed if her father's ship overtook them before she reached Venice, he would put her on a ship home immediately and she wouldn't even see Venice from a distance, let alone study here."

Sara frowned. "I knew about the other ship. When I finally was free of her clothes and could catch my breath, I saw it bearing down. That's when I first felt the sense of dread. Later, we learned that it was her father's ship. But, Zina, she jumped overboard completely unprepared for the consequences. Would her father really have done that?"

"I'm not certain, but I believe he probably would have. He does not like being defied and to allow her even a moment in Venice would mean her defiance paid off. Ceres was willful and as stubborn as her father. She wouldn't have liked getting this close and being thwarted. But for what it's worth, Reese is heartbroken."

"I'm sorry. But since I am not Ceres, maybe the best thing is just to keep the secret."

"And stay here in Venice? You would be playing with fire then, girl. Word would eventually get back to him about the pretty little dark-haired English girl who married the Scottish shipbuilder. He would become apoplectic with rage if he found you'd been here the whole time, alive and married without his permission. You don't want that. Trust me on this, Reese Llewellyn is not a man to cross."

"So, we should tell him?"

"I don't know what the best course of action is. It is possible, if you went to him and told him about everything— I mean that you suffer from amnesia, not about the pocket watch—he would allow you to marry Ben. But you have no guarantee of that. If you want to be certain to marry Ben, it might be better for the two of you to leave Venice altogether. As we both know, Ceres is lost to him forever now and you're right, it might be better to leave it that way. But as I've said, you can't stay here if you do. It could be disastrous."

"You can't be serious."

"I am deadly serious. He could have you on a ship to England so fast it will make your head spin. Then you would be under his thumb forever. The chances that you could make it back here would be almost nil. Ceres managed once because he didn't expect it. You can bet he won't let it happen again. I wouldn't even put it past him to have Ben killed."

A cold chill passed over Sara. She knew Zina was right. Llewellyn did pose a serious threat. Perhaps not to Sara herself, but to Ben and she suspected possibly even to Zina.

Sara blinked back tears. "I'll talk to Ben about it. He would have to leave everything. I wouldn't want that. Maybe it's best if I return to my time."

Zina shook her head. "No Sara. Don't do anything rash. If I'm not much mistaken, Ben would not think twice about leaving everything to be with you. You would both be miserable for the rest of your lives if you are separated by time. And no matter what, just as Gertrude says, the universe will unfold as it should."

~ * ~

Ben's morning had been frustrating. He learned there were two ways to be married legally. A priest could post banns for three consecutive Sundays, or they could obtain a wedding license. It seemed simple enough, but the devil was in the details.

They could be married immediately with a wedding license. However, Sara Wells was twenty-seven years old, but Ceres Llewellyn was barely nineteen and she looked it. If a girl was under twenty-one, in order for her to get a marriage license, she had to have her parent or guardian's consent. They could say her parents were deceased, but she still would have had a guardian of some sort. And no one would believe she was older than twenty-one. Furthermore, if they lied and the marriage was later challenged, it could be invalidated.

To be married after posting banns was easier in some respects. An underage bride did not have to prospectively have the consent of a parent or guardian. But, if a parent or guardian stepped forward to object while the banns were posted, there could be no marriage.

The problem with posting the banns was that their plans to marry wouldn't remain clandestine. Which, in truth, was the reason for posting banns. But considering that Benedict was marrying a girl about whom no one knew anything, it would doubtlessly raise curiosity about who she was. If talk reached Llewellyn's ears, that might be disastrous. Of course, Benedict could talk to the priest. He might be able to convince the man not to go strictly by the book and marry them anyway. That too was risky but Benedict decided it was the best option.

That was until he arrived at the shipyard. He had barely reached his office when his partner entered with a sheet of paper in his hand and shut the door. Emilio was more than just his partner, he was a dear friend. In fact, he'd been like a father to Benedict ever since his parents had left for Scotland. The solemn expression on his face had told Benedict something was seriously wrong.

"Sit down, Emilio. What's the matter?"

"My young friend, I am worried."

"About what?"

"About you."

"Me? I'm fine. Things are great in fact."

"I've noticed. Others have as well. That's why I'm worried."

"I don't understand."

"A month ago, you decided not to come to the shipyard for a week. You've never done that."

"I know, but I finished the drawings we'd discussed during that time."

"Yes, you did. And they are brilliant as usual, but that's not the point. You were away from the shipyard for a week. Then when you did come in, you seemed different. Happier. You no longer took your dinner in the middle of the day, but rushed home in the evening. To what? I asked myself. My wife suggested that you might have finally found a nice girl. 'No, Concetta,' I said. 'Benedict would tell me if he had.' She said, 'give him time.' So, I did. Now three weeks have passed and not only are you still acting like a

209

man in love, I am beginning to hear whispers. You have been seen on occasion with a young lady in your gondola. So, I asked myself, 'why would he keep this a secret?'"

"Emilio, I…"

"Then this morning the answer hit me. Reese Llewellyn has posted notices offering a substantial reward to anyone who can give him information regarding his lost daughter." Emilio read from the leaflet in his hand. "*On July ninth my darling daughter, Ceres, fell overboard as the ship on which she traveled neared Venice. Articles of clothing belonging to her were found, but not her body. She has a small build, black hair, and blue eyes. Her devoted father still prays to find her alive and is offering ten ducats to anyone with reliable information as to her whereabouts and five hundred ducats to anyone who returns her to him alive and well.*"

Emilio looked up from the leaflet. "It occurred to me that you stayed at home the week starting July tenth. It also occurred to me if that girl did survive, the nearest bit of land would be the Lido."

Silence hung between them for a moment.

"Benedict, did you find this girl? Are you in love with her?"

Benedict swallowed hard. He couldn't lie to Emilio.
"Yes. But there's a bit more to it. When I found her she
didn't remember who she was. She thought her name was
Sara. I offered to see what I could find out, but she begged
me not to. She said she was afraid. She believed something
terrible would happen if I asked questions."

"But when you returned to the office the following
week, the news of Llewellyn's daughter was everywhere.
You had to know this Sara you found was actually Ceres
Llewellyn."

"I did. And I went home that evening and told her
that her father was looking for her. Then she told me a story I
could scarcely believe. But Emilio I do believe it." He
proceeded to tell his partner about Sara Wells and the pocket
watch.

When he was through, Emilio asked, "You believe
that story?"

"I do. When you meet her, you'll understand why.
She is unlike any girl I've ever met. And we didn't tell her
father because she believed it would be kinder. She isn't
Ceres and if she were returning to her own time, Ceres's
body will die here anyway."

"*If* she were returning to her own time?"

"We are in love, Emilio. She wants to stay here with me. I've asked her to marry me."

"This is all nearly impossible to believe. But you are a good man, a smart man who is not easily hoodwinked. I can only trust that your faith in her is well placed. But having said that, you can't keep this secret any longer. If I put it all together, others might. Five hundred ducats is an immense amount of money. Hell, for that matter, ten ducats is as well. It would be better for you to go to Llewellyn and explain what happened. I don't mean about the watch, but explain about her losing her memory and that you only just put the pieces together. Tell him you wish to marry her."

"I've considered that. But I don't know what I'd do if he rejected the proposal. Emilio, she is my soulmate. I cannot risk losing her. I thought there might be less chance of that if I married her first."

"Ah, ask forgiveness instead of permission?"

Benedict nodded.

"I can't believe that would be necessary. He's a reasonable man. He couldn't possibly find a better husband for her. You are a partner in an extremely successful shipbuilding business and a fine young man with no vices to speak of. Furthermore, he will get discounts on every ship he commissions from us for the rest of his life."

"It seems I have very little choice anyway. She's only nineteen so I can't get a license without his permission. We don't need permission to be married by a priest, but the banns will have to be posted. When news of this bounty spreads, it's too much to hope that he wouldn't hear something. If you'll excuse me, I should go talk with Sara about this immediately."

As Benedict left, Emilio put a hand on his shoulder. "As I said, you are fine young man. Her father would be a fool to refuse your offer of marriage. But you do have one other marriage option."

"What's that?"

"The captain of a vessel can legally marry a couple at sea. If you think the only way to have her as your wife is to flee, I will assist you in any way possible."

"Thank you, Emilio."

Benedict had collected her from Zina's. It didn't bode well that his normally cheerful Sara looked tense and upset.

"Were you able to get a license?" She asked, her tone strained.

"No. But we'll talk about it at home."

When they had reached the privacy of their kitchen, it became immediately clear that neither of them had good news.

Nothing to Lose

Sara paced, wringing her hands. "Ben, what are we going to do? Zina says we should flee. She doesn't believe Llewellyn will receive this well. But you've built a wonderful business here. I can't ask you to leave it."

He stood, wrapping his arms around her to stop her pacing. "Nothing is more important to me than you. However, Emilio believes Llewellyn is reasonable and will see the advantages this match will have for him."

"The things Zina said about his temper are certainly consistent with the dread I feel from Ceres."

"We can flee then. I will go into Venice tomorrow and discuss the business with Emilio. He may be willing to buy me out. That would give us funds to start over somewhere else. I can also find out what options we have to leave Venice."

Sara nodded, resting her head against his chest. "It's just I worry that I am lending too much weight to Ceres's fears. Zina said something that concerns me. She said Llewellyn adored Ceres and gave her everything she ever desired. She said it wasn't surprising that Ceres rebelled the first time he said no to her."

"Why does that concern you?"

"Just that much of what we've done concerning Llewellyn has been based on what I believe Ceres feels, but that doesn't mean she's right. I worry that I'm putting too much faith in an over-indulged teenager. What if she's wrong? What if her father will rejoice in finding her and like Mr. Santi says, welcome a marriage proposal from you?"

"So putting Ceres's feelings aside, Zina too is concerned about him."

"But Mr. Santi isn't. He knows Llewellyn as a businessman. Zina knows him as someone who pays for her companionship. There is a power gradient there that could be driving her opinion."

Benedict kissed the top of her head. He wanted Sara as his wife more than he wanted his next breath. The only way to ensure that would happen would be to flee with her and never look back. But she seemed so conflicted he didn't know what the best path was. "Sara, what does your gut tell you?"

"That honesty is always best."

He nodded. "Then I will go to see Llewellyn tomorrow."

"Not alone. I'm going too."

He shook his head. "I'm not sure that's a good idea."

"He won't believe I've lost all of my memories if he doesn't see and talk to me."

Benedict tried to dissuade her over the course of the evening but ultimately agreed that their best chance at the honest approach was to go together.

Chapter 17

The next morning, he and Sara crossed the lagoon to the Arsenale. He helped her alight from the gondola and took her up to the offices of Santi and MacIan. Just as he knew she would, Sara charmed Emilio.

With the pleasantries aside, Benedict told his partner their plan to talk to Llewellyn.

Emilio looked relieved. "I'm glad to hear it. I don't want to lose you as a partner and this is really the only way to avoid that."

"How shall I do it then?" Benedict asked.

Emilio considered it for a moment. "I think we should go to his home here in Venice."

Benedict arched an eyebrow. "We?"

His old friend smiled. "Yes, Benedict. I have known Reese Llewellyn longer than you have. I will go with you, to vouch for your character."

Benedict was touched. This might not go particularly well and Emilio had to know that. But he would stand with them anyway. "Thank you. I owe you so much."

"Benedict, I've always thought of you as the son I never had. You owe me nothing. It's what a father would do."

Benedict didn't know what to say. "Thank you."

Emilio smiled. "Just make me godfather to your first child."

They waited until a bit later in the morning before seeking Llewellyn out at his home. He didn't live far from San Marco, but not on a canal. They moored the gondola near the Doge's palace and walked the rest of the way.

A servant answered the door.

Emilio addressed him. "Good morning. I'm Emilio Santi and I would like to speak with Mr. Llewellyn."

The servant looked past him at Benedict and Sara. His eyes went wide. "Yes, *Signore*. Please come in."

He showed them to the receiving room and excused himself. "I'll tell *Signore* Llewellyn you're here."

Benedict began to worry that this had been a mistake. As brave as Sara had been about this and as sure as she was that it was the right course, now she looked terrified. He took hold of her hand. "I love you Sara."

She gripped his hand and turned her frightened eyes to his. "I love you too, Ben. With all my heart."

Before Benedict told her he was sure everything would be all right, Reese Llewellyn entered the room.

"My God. Ceres, I can't believe it. I had all but lost hope." He pulled her into a hug, breaking Benedict's connection to her.

"Santi, I don't know how you did this, but thank you. Ceres, little one, where have you been."

"She's been with me, Mr. Llewellyn," said Benedict.

"Why has it take you so long to return her to me?"

Sara extricated herself from Llewellyn's grip. "Because, when he found me, I had no memories of my life before going overboard. I couldn't tell him who I was because I didn't remember. I still don't."

"What do you mean? Ceres, of course you remember who you are."

"I'm sorry, sir, but I don't. I thought my name was Sara. That's what I told Benedict. He didn't know I was your daughter."

"You've been with Benedict MacIan this entire time?"

"Yes. He's been very kind to me."

"Then you have my thanks, MacIan. I thought my daughter was lost to me. I understand now why it's taken so long. I'll see that you're given the reward money."

Benedict bristled. "Sir, I don't want the reward money."

"Of course you do. You've done me a great service and I owe it to you."

"Sir, I've become very fond of Sara—Ceres that is. The only thing I seek from you is her hand in marriage."

"Her hand in marriage?"

Sara nodded her head. "And I want to marry him…Father."

Llewellyn took her hand in his, patting the back of it. "My darling, you're confused."

"No, I'm not. I love him."

Benedict stepped forward. "Yes, sir. And I love her with all my heart. As you are aware, I'm a partner in Santi and MacIan. She would want for nothing."

"Llewellyn, we've known each other for many years," said Emilio.

"That we have. The finest ships in my fleet were built by Santi and MacIan."

Emilio smiled broadly. "And just imagine the many more that we'll build for you. You will never again pay what other merchants do for our ships. You will be family. And I can assure you, there is no finer young man in Venice that

Benedict MacIan. He will make an excellent husband for Ceres."

"I can't thank you both enough for caring for her and returning her to me."

Benedict became acutely aware of the fact that Llewellyn hadn't responded to any of the three of them regarding his proposal. "Sir, may I have Ceres's hand in marriage?"

Llewellyn picked up a bell and ringing it. "MacIan, my daughter has been through quite a bit. I'm not certain decisions of this magnitude should be made at such a time."

A servant stepped into the room. "You rang, *Signore*?"

"Yes, Eduardo. This is my daughter Ceres." He kissed the back of her hand. "Please see that she's made comfortable in one of the guest rooms."

Sara jerked her hand away from him. "No. I'm not staying here. I'm marrying Benedict." She crossed the room and wrapped her arms around Benedict.

Benedict put an arm around her. "Sir, please, you haven't answered my proposal. May we have your blessing to marry?" He intentionally did not ask permission again.

Llewellyn's eyes narrowed and he clenched his jaw. Benedict glimpsed the temper that Zina had warned Sara about. "Gentlemen, I would prefer to discuss this privately. I don't want to upset my daughter."

"I'm already upset and I'm not leaving," declared Sara.

"Ceres, my darling—"

"No. Benedict has cared for me these last few weeks. I owe him my life and I love him. You even acknowledge that you are in his debt."

"I am grateful he helped you when you needed him. And I understand that you believe you are in love with him. I will happily pay him the reward I offered for your safe return. And had it been nearly anyone else, I probably would have given my permission. But make no mistake, I will *never* allow my daughter to marry a savage Scot. *Never*. No matter how much it would benefit me. You will go home to England as soon as humanly possible." He took a stride toward them.

Emilio stepped between them. "You are being foolish, Llewellyn. You will never find a better husband for Ceres."

"A toad would be a better husband than a Scot," he roared. Then, addressing his servant he said, "Eduardo, send for the police."

"Don't bother," said Emilio. "We're leaving. Benedict, Sara, after you."

Llewellyn lunged at Emilio, throwing him to the ground before turning on Benedict.

Benedict let go of Sara, stepping in front of her to block her from Llewellyn. "Go now, Sara. Run."

In that moment, with Benedict's attention directed toward Sara, Llewellyn grabbed a heavy glass vase from a table and swung it at Benedict's head. He fell to his knees, blacking out when Llewellyn struck him with it again, full force.

~ * ~

Sara looked on with horror as Ceres's father attacked Mr. Santi. Then Ben shoved her away and told her to run. She did. She couldn't do anything to prevent what was happening and if Mr. Llewellyn got his hands on her, he could force her to board a ship and have her sailing to England on the next tide. She had to make certain that didn't happen. A servant tried to grab her as she reached the front door. She broke his grip and practically flew out of the house, running flat out towards the piazza, dodging people on the street. If she could reach the piazza, perhaps she could meld into the perpetual flow of people there.

Then, just before she reached the piazza, without making a conscious decision, she cut down a narrow side street and entered the first shop she came to. It was a lace shop that she had visited once before with Zina. She pretended to examine some lace shawls while making an effort not to appear as winded as she was. The lady running the shop gave her a quizzical look.

Sara fanned herself with her hand. "It's an exceedingly warm day."

The matron nodded. "It is indeed. Is there something I can assist you with?"

Come to think of it, a veil or shawl that she could use to conceal herself a bit with wouldn't go astray. But she carried no money and she was certain Benedict didn't have an account here. "Well…I…"

A light of recognition showed in the woman's face and she smiled broadly. "Ah, yes, I remember you now. You work for Signora Peretti. I have her order in the back. I won't be a minute."

Holy God, what was she going to do now? She wasn't here to pick up Zina's lace goods. Maybe she should just leave before the woman returned. Then it occurred to her that she had nowhere to go. She couldn't pilot the gondola. She had no money to pay a gondolier and even if she did, Benedict's house would be the first place Llewellyn might look for her. She knew no one at the shipyard from whom she could seek help and she felt sure Llewellyn would check there as well. The only other place she could go would be the last place he'd think to look—his courtesan's home. *The universe certainly does unfold as it should, Gertrude.*

The woman came out of the back room with a paper wrapped bundle. "Here you are. Is there anything else you need?"

"Thank you." Sara took the bundle from her and glanced down at the shawls again. She picked up a light pinkish-beige shawl made out of a thin cotton lawn and trimmed with wide lace. "Actually, I'd like to add this to the order." There were several beautiful lace fans displayed on another table. A fan would be nearly as good as a mask at hiding her face. She picked one up. "And this too, please."

The woman smiled. "I'll wrap the shawl, but I expect the fan might be a blessing on a day such as this."

Sara smiled. "Yes. Thank you very much."

"Are these for you or *Signora* Peretti?"

"They are for the *signora*. Can you put them on her account?" Sara knew Zina wouldn't mind and Ben would pay her back as soon as they were out of this mess.

"Yes, certainly."

"Thank you." Sara made a slight bow.

"You're very welcome."

Nothing to Lose

Sara stepped out of the shop, continued down the lane to the first alley, and ducked into it. She made her way through to the next little street. She wasn't sure exactly where she was, but if she could find her way to the Grand Canal, within sight of the Rialto Bridge or even the church of San Silvestri, she could find Zina's house. She unwrapped the shawl and covered her head and part of her face with it. Then, with Zina's package in one hand and the fan in the other, she wound her way through the streets and alleys heading generally to the northwest.

After a few wrong turns and dead ends, she reached the Grand Canal just south of the Rialto Bridge, not far from the little alley she had imagined to be time portal a month ago. She breathed a sigh of relief, turned to the left, and walked until she reached the place across the canal from San Silvestri where she and Ben had ended up on Saturday night. From here she knew exactly where to go.

When she arrived at Zina's house, she knocked at the door to the street entrance. Zina's butler, Mauricio, seemed surprised to see her there. "Your friend didn't bring you by gondola?"

Sara indicated the package in her hand. "I had a bit of shopping to do first."

The man smiled. "Ah yes, I see. The *signora* is in the drawing room. Follow me."

Sara hesitated a moment. "Is she alone?"

He frowned. "Yes. I would consult with her first were she not."

Sara gave a nervous laugh. "Of course, you would. That was silly of me."

He led her through the house to the drawing room. "*Signora* Peretti, Miss Wells is here to see you."

Zina's eyes went wide for a moment, but she covered her surprise quickly. "Sara, dear, do come in and sit down."

The butler asked, "Will I bring tea, *Signora*?"

She nodded, "Yes, thank you, Mauricio."

He closed the door behind him as he left.

"What's wrong? What are you doing here?"

"Oh, Zina—," She burst into tears.

Zina rushed to her, gathering Sara in her arms. "Sara, darling, tell me what's wrong. I'm certain we can fix it."

Sara swallowed hard and dashed at the tears on her face, trying to regain some control. "We told him."

"Who? Llewellyn?"

"Yes. Ben and I discussed it for what must have been hours yesterday. As it turns out, while I was here with you, Ben learned that Llewellyn was offering a significant reward for information about me. *Signore* Santi put all the pieces together and was concerned that others would, too. He believed Llewellyn would understand about the amnesia and ultimately see the advantages of a marriage for me with Ben."

"And he didn't?"

"Oh, he believed us about the amnesia, but he refused to allow the marriage. He said he wouldn't marry me to a 'savage Scot' no matter how it benefitted him. He said he probably would have granted permission to anyone else."

"Sara, I'm so sorry. I didn't realize Reese held such a prejudice or I'd have told you. What happened after he refused you?"

"We tried to leave. Signore Santi put himself between Llewellyn and us to give us a chance to get away. But Llewellyn threw him to the floor and went for Ben. Ben told me to run and I did."

"Well, it's a good thing you did. If you'd played the fool and tried to save Ben, the chances are extremely good that you would already be on a ship to England."

"But what do we do now?" A horrible thought occurred to her. "He wouldn't have killed Ben, would he?"

"Not in his home, by his own hand. He can bribe his way out of a lot of things, but not murder. If he wants Ben dead, he'll make sure it can't be connected to him. No, I suspect he's just had him arrested."

"On what charges? He hasn't done anything wrong."

"Sara, he's kept you in his home for nearly a month. I suspect Reese would levy the same charges as those against Casanova, *an affront to common decency.*"

"But we haven't...that is not until after the ball..."

Zina smiled. "So, in fact you *have*. But it wouldn't matter anyway. He doesn't need Ben convicted. He just needs him imprisoned long enough to find you and get you out of Venice. But don't worry. He won't find you."

"What about Ben and *Signore* Santi?"

"I will send a servant to learn all he can about them. After we know the lay of the land, we can put a plan together."

The mention of sending a servant awakened another fear. If one of them spoke to Llewellyn, it might put Zina in danger simply for trying to help. "Zina, maybe it's better if I just leave. If your servants know who I am, one of them might go to Llewellyn. It could put you in danger."

Zina shook her head. "My servants are loyal to me."

"But what about the reward money?"

Zina laughed. "Reese already pays my servants to spy on me. I pay them more not to. I have never done anything of which he would disapprove but that isn't the point. My business is my own."

"But five hundred ducats is a huge sum."

"Sara, stop worrying. If one of my servants was tempted by that money, the seven-hundred and fifty ducats I would pay them to keep quiet would tempt them more. Besides, they know if they broke my confidence, they would never work in a fine Venetian home again."

Sara nodded, but frowned. She couldn't help but worry. If all was lost and Ben was killed, she could still say the word and return to her own time. But if she did that, Zina would be the one left to deal with the mess.

Zina cocked her head to one side. "You don't believe me?"

Before Sara could answer, Mauricio had returned with tea.

Zina smiled. "Let me prove it to you, Sara." She turned her attention to the butler. "Mauricio, do you know who this is?"

"Miss Sara Wells, *Signora*."

"No, I mean do you know who she *really* is?"

"Well, there has been a bit of speculation, *Signora*. It appears that she could be Miss Ceres Llewellyn. She first appeared shortly after Miss Llewellyn was lost and she bears a reasonable resemblance to *Signore* Llewellyn."

Sara gasped.

Zina laughed. "Well spotted, Mauricio. I didn't put those two bits of information together immediately. Are you aware of the reward being offered for her return?"

He nodded once. "Most everyone in the household is, *Signora*."

"Good. Now, Mauricio, you must recognize Sara is very new here. She doesn't understand the way of things. Is there any chance that *Signore* Llewellyn will discover that she is my guest here?"

"Only if the lady herself tells him."

"Would you mind explaining why that is true to her?"

"Not at all, *Signora*. Miss Wells, it is simple. We, *Signora* Peretti and everyone working in her household, are Venetians. Mr. Llewellyn is not. While he comes to town once every few months, we must live here for the rest of our lives. He might offer a huge amount of money for a single piece of information, but once he has it, there is no more income to be had. On the other hand, the *Signora* is a very benevolent employer. She pays her people generously and is loyal to them. May I offer an example, *Signora*?"

Zina nodded her consent.

"Miss Wells, the butler who worked for the *Signora* before me suffered a terrible accident. He fell a great distance and his injuries left him unable to walk—thus unable to work. She still pays him a pension so he can care for his family. So you see, Miss Wells, we know we can absolutely count on her. No amount of Llewellyn's money is worth losing her trust."

Sara nodded. "Thank you for telling me, Mauricio."

"It was my pleasure." He gave a small bow.

"So, Mauricio," said Zina, "I need for someone to investigate something for me." She explained quickly about *Signore* Santi and Benedict.

"Certainly, *Signora*. May I suggest that Miss Wells retire to the green bedroom? *Signore* Llewellyn tends to seek you out when he is not having the best of days."

"You are absolutely right. I'll show her there myself."

Chapter 18

When Benedict awoke, he was certain he'd died and gone to hell. His head throbbed and he lay face down on a wooden floor. The heat of the room was almost unbearable. He rolled to his side and pushed up into a sitting position to look around. The light was dim but he could see that he was in some sort of low-ceilinged cell, perhaps twelve feet square.

"You've rejoined the living," said a voice behind him.

Benedict turned at the sound, causing his head to swim.

"Easy there, man. The ambiance of these stellar accommodations will not be improved by the contents of your stomach." The man was perhaps older than Benedict by a year or two. He wore only breeches and had a long beard.

"Where are we?"

"The Leads. One of the cells under the lead roof of the Ducal palace. I'm Giacomo Casanova. Who are you?"

This is the infamous libertine, Casanova? "My name is Benedict MacIan."

"Pleased to make your acquaintance, Benedict MacIan. But I'm still left wondering who you are."

"I don't understand. I told you, I'm Benedict MacIan."

"That's only your name. *Who are you?* They only put prisoners from the upper classes in the Leads. I am fairly well acquainted with the Venetian aristocracy and the wealthier members of the merchant class. Your name is familiar, but I can't place you and I'm certain we've never met. Which can only mean if you have money, you don't spend it on the usual pastimes."

"I am a partner in a shipbuilding company, Santi and MacIan."

"Ah, yes. That MacIan. So tell me, MacIan, what did you do to wind up here?"

"Nothing."

"Yes, that's rather common up here. We've all done nothing. So perhaps you'd like to tell me what they *think* you've done."

"Honestly, I'm not sure."

"Tell me what happened immediately before you were clocked on the head and maybe we can figure it out together." Casanova's tone dripped with sarcasm.

"I was at *Signore* Llewellyn's home."

"That one has a nasty temper I've heard. Did you cheat him—or, that is, did you and he disagree on the quality of your craftsmanship?"

"No. It was nothing like that." If he was going to tell Casanova the story, he had to stick to what they'd told Llewellyn. "I live on the Lido. About a month ago, I found a girl on the beach."

"Just sitting by the sea? Do you often find girls on the sands of the Lido? If so, I must consider making a home there."

Benedict shook his head, a little frustrated. "She wasn't 'just sitting there.' She had nearly drowned. She thought her name was Sara but couldn't remember anything else, not even how she'd ended up in the water. I took care of her. We fell in love."

"Of course you did. But how does Llewellyn figure in this?"

"I learned that his daughter had fallen overboard just as her ship approached Venice. Clothing belonging to her was found, but not her body. He believed she was alive. Based on all the evidence, I believed that my Sara was actually Ceres Llewellyn. I took her to him, accompanied by my partner, Emilio Santi. I asked for her hand in marriage."

"Sounds like a match made in heaven. Or perhaps a banker's office. What could be better for a merchant than to marry his daughter to a well-reputed shipbuilder?"

"That's what Emilio and I both thought, but Llewellyn refused."

"Why? Hell, I'd marry you to my daughter, except I don't have one…that I know of at least."

"He said he'd never marry her to a *savage Scot*."

"Well, he has a point there."

Benedict glared at him.

Casanova smiled and shrugged. "'Twas only a jest. You don't seem all that savage to me, although you are undeniably a Scot. But we digress. What happened after he refused you?"

"We attempted to leave. Llewellyn attacked Santi. I told Sara to run but in that instant, Lewellyn struck me in the head with something. Then I woke up here."

"And the lovely Sara or Ceres or whatever her name is?"

"I don't know what happened to her."

"Well, for the moment, let's hope she did run or your chances of ever seeing her again are dismal. Now, you say you've kept her for a month. Is she carrying your child?"

"No. It wasn't like that. We didn't…"

"You didn't? Why on earth not? How could you possibly know you love each other?" Casanova waved a hand. "It doesn't really matter. The fact is, no one in Venice, most certainly not her father, will believe you didn't avail yourself of her charms. Therefore, I suspect once you were incapacitated, he had you arrested and charged with *an affront to common decency*. One of the crimes, I'm sad to say, which landed me here."

Benedict put his throbbing head in his hands. "How am I going to get out of this?"

"You haven't been tried yet and you clearly aren't destitute. Bribes work rather well."

"I suspect Llewellyn is significantly better at that game than I am."

"No doubt. But one never knows what miracle might transpire."

~ * ~

By that evening, Sara had reason to hope. Zina's servant had learned that Ben had been arrested and charged with an affront to common decency on the grounds that he had despoiled Ceres Llewellyn.

Emilio Santi was not arrested. Aside from the fact that he had done nothing wrong, he was a well-respected member of Venetian society. In fact, he had almost convinced the chief of police to arrest Llewellyn for assaulting him. But in the end, the chief probably stood to gain more from Llewellyn than from Santi, so he didn't make the arrest.

Ben was being held in the Leads while he awaited trial. *Signore* Santi was working through legal channels to effect Ben's release.

She went to sleep that night hoping to be reunited with Ben the next day.

Llewellyn had called on Zina that evening and Sara stayed quietly ensconced in the green bedroom until he left the next morning. Once he was well gone, Zina filled her in and Sara's hopes plummeted.

"Reese spent most of the evening ranting about the day's events. However, he also bragged about spreading around enough money to secure a rapid conviction."

"*No*. How can he say he loves his daughter and do that to the man she loves?"

"I asked him the same thing. But he's convinced that she's too young to know anything about love and once she's away from Venice, she'll get over it."

"Do you think it will work? Will he get Ben convicted?"

Zina smiled. "No, I don't think so. You see, I have contacts of my own. Reese also dropped a tidbit of information that will be incredibly useful. Apparently, they've put Ben in a cell with Giacomo Casanova."

"How is that helpful?"

"Casanova and I have a mutual benefactor, Count Bragadin. Other than a lawyer, the prisoners in the Leads are not allowed visitors, but I have reason to believe Bragadin has a way of communicating with Casanova. I will pay a visit to the Count this morning. He'll know if there is something that can be done, and at the very least will enable us to send messages to Ben. Casanova himself may have some insight as to the best way to proceed."

Zina was true to her word and Count Bragadin promised to find out what he could.

Later that day, *Signore* Santi had called on Zina at her request. When he arrived, he was enormously relieved to find Sara there.

Sara jumped straight to the issue at hand. "What news do you have, *Signore*?"

"Unfortunately, it isn't as good as I'd hoped."

"What's happened?"

"Nothing. Not yet anyway. I have discussed the situation with our attorney. He tells me that Llewellyn has contacts in the judiciary. He fears if Benedict is taken to trial, he will be convicted. So our lawyer is working to try to have the charges dropped."

Sara covered her mouth with her hand, trying not to cry.

Zina put an arm around her. "Don't despair yet, Sara. It seems the route forward is obvious. We will let the lawyer do what he does best, but we will plan for a contingency. If he can't get the charges dropped, we simply need to get Ben out of prison before he goes to trial."

"How is that possible?"

A slow smile spread across Zina's face. "My dear, Llewellyn may have friends in high places, but sometimes friends in low places are equally, if not more, valuable. The guards in the ducal prison are paid a shockingly low salary. There is always an opportunity to improve their lives, for which they are not only grateful, but often seem to suffer temporary blindness. I will see what can be done tomorrow.

~ * ~

Zina's news the next afternoon buoyed Sara's spirits a good deal.

"The information from Count Bragadin is excellent. He had to *improve the lives* of several people to be able to contact Casanova but what he learned is very good news indeed."

"Is Ben all right?"

"It seems so. He has a bit of a headache as you might imagine, but he is otherwise fine. As luck would have it, it seems that Casanova has already been working on a way to escape and his plans are nearing completion. He paused work on it for fear that Ben was a spy, but Bragadin has vouched for him. The problem is, once the work is completed, his escape route will take him out of the cells, but not all of the way out of the castle. We need some inside help for that. I've greased a good few palms to ensure their way will be clear."

"When can we do this? Tonight?"

Zina shook her head. "No. It will take a bit of planning. First, we need to check with *Signore* Santi to see how things are coming on the legal front. The Count believes, if it's possible, it would be much better for Benedict to have the charges dropped and be released than it would be for him to escape."

"But what if they aren't dropped, or things drag on forever?"

"We won't let that happen. We will put things in place for the escape to occur next week regardless." Zina flashed a quick grin. "Casanova grows weary in prison. He has four more years to go on his sentence, but he's decided a year is quite long enough. Everyone concerned believes the best opportunity for the escape to be successful is to attempt it on a holiday. The feast of the Assumption is only five days away and the day after that is St. Rocco's feast day. Two holidays back-to-back will be even better. They will make their escape from the cells the night of the Assumption and will be free from the palace early in the morning of St. Rocco's day."

"Then what?"

"We will have to speak with *Signore* Santi about that, for we'll need his assistance. I've sent a message requesting he come here tomorrow."

Sara could scarcely sleep that night. If Benedict was caught escaping from prison, he could be in prison for a very long time. She prayed that the legal maneuvers would work. But sleep eluded her as she couldn't stop imagining one tragic scenario after another.

In the message Zina had sent to *Signore* Santi, she had suggested he time his visit fairly early in the day, as it would ensure that he and Llewellyn would not meet. It was unlikely Reese would visit before midday.

When pleasantries had been exchanged and they had taken seats in the drawing room, Emilio shared his news. "My lawyer says he is still hopeful he will be able to get the charges dropped."

"There's a 'but' hovering at the end of that sentence," said Zina.

He nodded. "But hopeful is one thing and confident is another. Sadly, he is not confident. He did say he was certain it won't happen today, nor will it happen over the weekend. The decision will be made Monday at the earliest."

Sara's heart fell.

Zina said, "Then we will just have to plan for the worst. Tuesday is the Feast of the Assumption. We'll put the necessary preparations in place to facilitate their escape."

Signore Santi nodded. "I agree. What else is needed?"

Zina answered, "I have everything arranged up to the moment they walk out the door. After that, we will need to get them out of the city. Casanova believes a gondola will be sufficient. And it probably is for him. But Ben and Sara will need more. I suspect the best course of action is to book passage for them on a ship that has no connection to Llewellyn, which will leave as soon as they are aboard Wednesday morning."

"It may be a challenge but I'll see that it's done."

Zina's brows drew together. "*Signore*, I don't wish to put undue stress on you, but if you think there is the remotest chance that the charges against Ben will be dropped and he will be released, you need to have similar arrangements in place for Monday."

"If he is released on Monday, can't we just wait until Wednesday to leave?" asked Sara.

"On Wednesday, it may take a while for the escape to be discovered and then for news of it to reach Reese. It's likely we'll have a few hours' cushion. But if Ben is released on Monday, Reese will know as soon as it happens—if not before—and he will be furious. If we dawdle at all, it will give him time to act. I have no doubt he'll be out for blood. We have to get both of you out of his reach immediately."

Sara could scarcely believe what she was hearing. It was bad enough that Benedict had lost his freedom and would lose his home and his business because of her. Now he was at risk of losing his life. She put her head in her hands.

Signore Santi patted her shoulder. "Don't worry. We'll free him and get you both well away from Reese Llewellyn."

244

"But where can we go? When we were considering not telling him about us, but just leaving Venice, Ben mentioned returning to Scotland."

"You can't do that now," said Zina. "That is far too close to Reese's base of power and he would expect Ben to go there."

Signore Santi nodded. "And you can't go to any major European port, at least not for long. When he fails to find you in Venice or Scotland, he will look further afield, Naples, Genoa, Marseille, Barcelona, Lisbon, none of them would be safe. You might consider smaller ports, like Dubrovnik, Cadiz, or Saint-Nazaire."

Zina shook her head. "Maybe in the short term, but I don't believe any European port will be safe for long. Reese is a man who holds grudges. He will believe that Benedict has stolen his precious daughter from him and will never stop looking to exact revenge."

"Then where do you suggest?" he asked.

"The colonies," she said simply.

Signore Santi shook his head. "No. That is British territory. He might not start looking there, but he surely will eventually. And once he does, he'll be able to find them easy enough. Plus, he'll have his own legal system on his side."

A smile spread across Zina's face, and for the first time that morning Sara smiled too.

Signore Santi frowned. "What amuses you both?"

"*Signore*," said Sara, "I know you are familiar with how I came to be here."

"Yes."

She glanced at Zina, silently asking for her permission to reveal that she too was a time traveler. Zina nodded. "Well, Zina and I didn't just happen to meet and become friends. Gertrude introduced us because Zina too used the watch a number of years ago and stayed here."

Santi looked shocked. "There are more of you?"

Zina shrugged. "Evidently. However, back to your question, the colonies are not always going to be under British control. If Ben and Sara change their surname, I think the chances are very slim that Llewellyn will be able to locate them ever. And in a matter of years, the British will be out and he'll have no legal recourse, so it won't matter."

He smiled. "Then I suspect that is the best choice in the long-run. Now, there is one other thing to discuss. Sara, the two of you will need funds to set up a new life and I find myself in a position to be able to buy out my partner. I will make the necessary arrangements. I will also have someone pack up what they can from Benedict's home—clothing and personal items and so forth. I'll see that it's all stowed on your ship."

Zina frowned. "Aren't you worried he might have Benedict's home watched?"

He shook his head. "I have spies of my own. His men did search the island but, coming up with nothing, haven't been back. It should be easy enough to get what they will need. Now, I have a bit of work ahead of me, so I'll take my leave. I don't believe I am being watched, but just in case, I probably shouldn't visit here again. I will send someone on Sunday who will fill you in on all the details of the arrangements I make."

~ * ~

On Sunday afternoon, Santi did send a messenger to tell them what plans had been made. If Benedict was released on Monday, he would be taken immediately to board a ship bound for Valencia, Spain. Santi would also have someone poised to take Sara to the ship.

But if Benedict wasn't released, the escape would ensue. Then on Wednesday morning, they would leave on a ship bound for Portugal. *Signore* Santi would make arrangements for Sara to board that ship well ahead of time on Tuesday. The captain of that vessel would keep her hidden until they sailed.

Finally, there would be a gondola awaiting *Signore* MacIan and *Signore* Casanova on Wednesday morning. It would first take Benedict into the harbor to the ship bound for Lisbon. Then *Signore* Casanova would be taken onward to the mainland, where a carriage had been arranged for him. Regardless of whether Sara and Benedict went to Spain or Portugal, they would be able to arrange passage onward to the colonies.

The entire situation worried Sara. The plan revolved around so many people it seemed impossible that it would remain a secret. She could only be vigilant and hope. She would not allow herself to be put on a ship for England.

Chapter 19

Benedict didn't quite know what to make of Giacoma Casanova. He had heard rumors about the infamous libertine. He assumed the man to be older and—well there was no other word for it—softer. In his experience men of Casanova's ilk had no great skills, did little to dirty their hands, and showed disdain to anyone who actually worked for a living.

However, Casanova surprised Benedict in many ways. It was true that the man was irreverent nearly to the point of blasphemy, and thus could maybe be accused of being an "affront to religion." In his manner of speaking, he also gave every impression of being indifferent to the plight of others, or even his own, but that was not borne out by his actions.

On Benedict's first night in the Leads, Casanova shared his dinner. "It's nearly certain they will bring you nothing tonight, and perhaps not tomorrow. I have a generous benefactor, Count Bragadin, who ensured I was given a stipend of sixty *soldi* per day. I have more than enough. You'll need to arrange for someone to bring you a bed and perhaps a chair. I can ask the Count to take care of it, if you wish."

"Arrange for furniture?"

"Yes. I'll give you a blanket to lay on and another to use as a pillow, but if you are here for more than a few days, you will want a bed at the very least."

Benedict didn't want to think of the possibility that he would be there more than one night, or maybe two. He hadn't committed a crime.

Over the next few days, Benedict found his cellmate to be well read and interesting to talk to, often displaying a wickedly funny, dry wit. It made the hours in the hellish heat tolerable.

The only thing that really confused Benedict seemed to happen every evening. After the guards had left in the evening, a scraping sound could be heard overhead. When Benedict first heard it, Casanova pretended that he could hear nothing. When Benedict insisted that something was scratching at the ceiling, Casanova acknowledged hearing the noise but credited it to rats.

"There are rats the size of rabbits here."

"By the almighty, if that sound is being made by rats, they'd need to be the size of ponies," countered Benedict.

"They are just loud rats. Believe me, who would know better than I? If they break through, we'll make saddles for them and ride out of here."

Then, after about four hours, the noise abruptly stopped, not starting again until the next evening.

On Friday, Benedict learned from his lawyer that Llewellyn had not been able to find his daughter since the incident.

"Is she safe?" asked Benedict.

The lawyer had glanced pointedly at Casanova before answering. "I certainly hope so, sir, but I would have no way of knowing. As I said, her father hasn't found her yet."

"MacIan, in case you didn't catch his meaning," said Casanova, "if he knows anything about Miss Llewellyn's whereabouts, he couldn't indicate that in front of me. I might be a spy. But I'm going to do you a favor. I'm going to turn my back. If he knows she is safe and well, he'll hold up one finger. If he doesn't know her whereabouts but she is assumed to be well, he'll hold up two fingers. If he truly knows nothing or is too cowardly to tell you, he'll shake his head. That way, you might get a meaningful answer and stop worrying. Although I fear that's a vain hope."

Casanova did turn his back and to Benedict's great relief the lawyer flashed one finger before saying, "I'm sorry, sir, as I said I have no way of knowing. However, I wanted you to know that I am trying to get the charges dropped. It's likely they'll make a determination on Monday."

Benedict sighed. He had slept on the floor for three nights so far, but he hadn't made arrangements for a bed because he'd believed he'd be leaving. Now faced with at least three more nights in this hell that was the Doge's prison, Benedict gave in and asked the lawyer to arrange for him to have a bed.

"Don't forget linens," said Casanova. "Ask for extra linens. You'll want two, maybe three sets."

It was on the tip of Benedict's tongue to tell his cellmate that he would certainly not need extra linens because he would be released soon, but he stopped himself. He had no idea of whether he would be released soon or not. And even if he was, Casanova still had nearly four years to serve on his sentence. It would be rude to rub that in, and he seemed very keen on getting those linens. If Benedict was released, he'd leave them behind. It was the least he could do.

On Monday, when his lawyer visited again, Benedict's hopes all but died.

"I'm sorry *Signore* MacIan, I was unable to convince the magistrate to drop the charges. You will stand trial on

Thursday, after the holy days. I have brought you a change of clothing so that you may look presentable while in court."

"You look exceedingly grim. Are you not confident about your abilities to prove me innocent?"

"No sir, I'm sorry to say, I am not."

"But I haven't done anything wrong."

"You despoiled Reese Llewellyn's daughter. And according to him, kept her locked away on your island. Once she was able, she ran from you and no one has been able to find her."

"Every word of that is false. We love each other. I intend to marry her."

"You can't prove that. And the young lady is not available to testify."

"But without her, he can't prove his story either."

"That's true, but he is well capable of bribing those he needs to in order to prevail. I'm very sorry, sir, but the best we can hope for on Thursday is a lenient sentence."

A bed and linens were brought to his cell that evening. He laid on it and stared at the ceiling.

"Cheer up, man. Perhaps your friends have been equally successful in bribing those needed to secure your release."

Somehow, Benedict doubted it.

He remained morose throughout the evening. Casanova had tried to pull him into conversation, but Benedict could only think about Sara and how he'd let her down. However, eventually the silence was almost more oppressive than the heat.

The silence?

He looked at Casanova. "Do you hear that?"

Casanova shook his head. "I hear nothing."

"That's want I mean. The scratching hasn't started."

"And it won't."

"Were the rats captured?" Benedict asked scathingly.

Casanova chuckled. "Now that I think on it, I don't believe that scratching was caused by rats at all."

"Are you finally going to tell me what it was?"

"As a matter of fact, I am. Several months ago, I was able to fashion a sharp spike out of a bolt I found. It was my plan to dig through the floorboards under my bed, drop into the gallery below, and escape. But my plan was thwarted when they found the hole. The moved me to this cell after that and as you are aware, they inspect every surface of it, every day."

"That would make it hard to dig through the floorboards again."

"It did. However, as fate would have it, I am acquainted with the prisoner whose cell is through that wall." He pointed. "His name is Father Balbi and I took advantage of an opportunity to smuggle my spike to him. He was able to make a whole in his ceiling, crawl over and dig into ours. The ceiling there is nearly paper thin now. Tomorrow night, when the city is celebrating the feast of the Assumption, he will climb out one last time, break a hole into our ceiling, and we shall all three escape."

"Escape? Are you serious? What if we are missed before we are fully away?"

"If that happened, our sentences would be doubled or tripled. But it won't happen. Llewellyn may be able to bribe judges, but the Count bribed everyone else who will be in this building tomorrow night. They will turn a blind eye to everything until the next morning."

Benedict was shocked. "This could actually work."

"Or we could get ourselves killed. Equal chances, I'd say."

"Why didn't you tell me about this from the start?"

"Mainly because I knew nothing about you and there was at least a possibility that the charges would be dropped. You might have been tempted to tell someone, if it meant your release."

"I wouldn't have done that."

"Yes, that's what my sources tell me."

"Your sources?"

"The less you know the better."

"Fair enough. Is there anything we need to do to prepare?"

"I'm not sure what we'll encounter on the way out. It would be helpful to have some strong rope. As luck would have it, you have a nice supply of extra linens. We can fashion the rope from those."

Benedict chuckled. "You had a plan."

Casanova shrugged. "A good plan never goes astray. It may fail, but it is still useful to have."

"Well then, let's get to it."

"You work on tearing the sheets into strips. Not too narrow, or they will be too weak. I'll tie the knots. A poorly tied knot could ruin us."

Benedict arched an eyebrow. "You know, I've worked around ships my entire life. I know a thing or two about tying knots."

"While that may be true, in some endeavors, specifically those that put my neck at stake, I feel the need to complete critical tasks myself."

As they worked to create the rope, a thought occurred to Benedict. "What will I do when we escape? I don't know where to go. I need to find Sara and get out of Venice, but I have no clue where she is."

"She will be waiting for you."

"Where, and for that matter, how, do you know that?"

"I'm not completely certain where she is now, but sometime tomorrow, she will be spirited aboard a ship that will set sail for Portugal the instant you are on it Wednesday morning. And I know because I have lines of communication not available to everyone."

"Did you know all of this earlier when my attorney was here?"

Casanova shrugged and nodded.

"And you went through that whole one finger two finger charade?"

"Oh, come on, that was fun. It made the man twitchy."

Benedict had to laugh.

Together he and Casanova worked until they had thirty feet of strong rope. It was rolled and hidden under Casanova's mattress by the next morning. His heart was lighter than it had been in days. Sara was safe and they'd be able to escape together.

~ * ~

By next evening, the full import of what they were about to do weighed on Benedict. This could go seriously wrong and be disastrous. He thought of Sara, the remarkable woman he loved with his whole being who had been brought to him across time. What had she said the old woman told her? *The universe unfolds as it should.* Aye, he and Sara had found each other against all odds. He would get through this night and hold her in his arms again. That was the thought he had to hold firmly on to.

At the usual time, after the guards were gone, the scraping on the ceiling started again.

"Time to pack, my friend." Casanova put a silk lined cloak on his bed and started laying his clothing on it."

Benedict frowned. "Pack? I have nothing to take but the rope."

"But you do. You need to take that fine suit your lawyer brought you."

"Why?"

Casanova shook his head as if he were dealing with a very slow child. "Because, MacIan, you look like a man who has been wearing the same clothes for days. Almost as if you have been in prison. If you happen to be seen after we leave, by someone who hasn't been paid to look away, we don't want to give them a reason to shout for the police. If we are dressed like gentleman, we could stop and have coffee in the piazza and no one would look at us twice."

What he said made sense, so as Casanova created a bundle of belongings and tore one of the remaining sheets to tie to the bundle as a strap. Benedict folded his suit and put it into a pillowcase, also creating a strap with a piece of torn sheet.

Before long, the ceiling cracked and a hole opened up. A small, bookish man stuck his head through it. "We need to be on our way gentlemen."

They climbed up through the hole, finding themselves in a low attic space immediately under the peak of the sloping roof. The only thing separating them from the outside world was the lead plates. Together Benedict and Casanova worked to lift the panel. Between them, they managed to loosen one edge and bend it until there was enough room to squeeze through.

Casanova stuck his head out and Benedict heard him swear.

"What's amiss?"

"The moon is bright and as it's a feast day, San Marco's square will be filled with people. It's too much to hope that we won't be seen illuminated by the damnable orb."

Father Balbi panicked. "We have to go. It'll be midnight soon."

"It'll be midnight in two hours," said Casanova dryly.

The priest was working himself into a state. "But we can't just stay here. There is no way to cover the damage to the cells now. We have to take our chances."

Benedict looked at Casanova. "How high is the moon? How long until it sets?"

"We have about four hours."

Benedict put a hand on Father Balbi's shoulder. "Father, no one will be back to check on the cells until after sunup. We will have six hours of darkness from when the moon sets until the sun rises. It is far better to wait here until we have a hope of not being seen."

It was perhaps the most nerve-wracking four hours of his life, made no better by Balbi's endless moaning about their imminent failure.

Finally, they were engulfed by darkness. They ventured out onto the roof, inching their way down, until they reached the gutter. The priest looked over the edge. "We should just jump into the canal and we'll be away."

"Have you lost your mind, old man?" asked Casanova. "We are much too high. That would mean nearly certain death."

Benedict looked over the edge. "I think I could climb down to that dormer. We could attempt to get in through it."

Casanova nodded. "It's worth a try."

Benedict climbed over the edge of the roof thinking he could hang from the edge and his feet would reach the dormer. But they didn't. *By all that's good and holy*. He was hanging by his fingers from the edge of the roof of the Doge's palace. The only thing he could do was let go and hope he could catch himself on the dormer roof. He uttered a quick prayer and dropped.

His feet hit the dormer and slipped to one side. He was falling and he grasped frantically, his fingers catching hold of the grate over the window. The grate, not intended to support the weight of a man swinging on it, began to loosen. Benedict managed to pull himself back onto the dormer before the grate gave way completely and fell into the canal.

Given that he was safe, he realized the grate giving way was actually a blessing. They couldn't have entered the window otherwise.

"That was rather impressive," said Casanova. "But Father Balbi here doesn't think he has quite your athletic ability."

Benedict snorted. He suspected that wasn't even close to what Father Balbi was saying. "I think I can break the window and get in. Then you can throw me the end of the rope. I'll secure it inside and you can hold it at that end. Put your feet in the gutter as a brace."

"There is no way I can support the good father's full weight."

"You don't have to. It's an easy enough drop if you don't have to worry about losing your balance. The rope is just there to grab as he hits the dormer. Neither of you will fall."

Casanova shook his head and said, "I believe you, thousands wouldn't," even as he was dropping the rope to Benedict.

Sitting on the roof of the dormer and using his heels, Benedict kicked in the glass, knocking as much of it out as he could before lowering himself off the roof, onto the sill, and into the room below. Wrapping the rope around his hand, he cleared the rest of the glass from the frame. Then he wrapped the rope around his body and braced himself against the wall. He called, "Ready when you are."

He felt the rope go taunt and then smiled as he heard Casanova arguing with Balbi. Finally, he heard the priest give a little cry, then heard the thunk of his feet hitting the dormer just as he felt the rope being yanked on. Since neither the priest nor Casanova went flying off the roof into the canal, he figured they were successful. He let go of the rope, leaned out the window, and helped Balbi climb in. Then he leaned out again, looking up at Casanova.

"It looks like I'll have to jump as you did."

"Yes, but tie the rope around your waist before you climb over the edge. I'll eliminate the slack before you drop and anchor this end. If you lose your balance the rope will catch you and we'll be able to pull you in."

"As much as I hate to do it, it's the only way."

Benedict wasn't completely certain that he could catch the weight of a falling man, even braced as he was, but he needn't have worried. Casanova dropped to the dormer and maintained his footing.

Once they were all safely inside, Casanova broke the lock on the door. "Stay here. I'll see if I can figure out where we are."

After a few minutes he came back, looking exceedingly well pleased. "This is a storage area on the highest level of the palace, well away from the prison cells.

Now we simply need to change our clothes and make our way downstairs. We should be able to simply walk out."

It seemed easy enough, but trying to find their way through palace corridors and down to the main level in the dark was more challenging than they expected. When they finally found themselves at an exit and pulled on the door, it was locked.

"We're doomed. We're doomed," cried Father Balbi, yanking at the locked door.

Moments later, a key turned in the lock and a guard opened the door. He smiled broadly at them. "Locked in, were you?" He stepped back holding the door for them. "Well, you can be on your way now."

"Thank you, sir," said Casanova as he strode confidently through the door and turned to walk towards the canal.

"Yes, thank you," said Benedict following Casanova.

The priest mumbled something unintelligible and practically ran past the guard.

"Where to now?" asked Benedict.

"I believe a gondola awaits us."

And sure enough, it did. They climbed into the gondola and were rowed away from San Marco. Before long, the gondolier steered towards a longboat in the lagoon.

To Benedict's great relief, Emilio Santi waited in the boat.

"This is where you leave us, MacIan," said Casanova. "I must say, the Lord and I have had a rather rocky relationship recently, but this adventure would never have been successful without your assistance. So, while I know the last few days were trying for you, I consider them a blessing." He offered Benedict his hand.

Benedict took it, shaking it firmly. "I suppose He isn't quite finished with either of us yet."

"I suppose not, but I fear I will continue to disappoint Him."

Benedict laughed. "Perhaps, but I understand He's the forgiving type."

"Let's hope so. Farewell, Benedict. Godspeed."

"Farewell, Giacomo. I hate to ask this, but I fear I must. If you ever find yourself in a position to tell the story of this unbelievable escape, would you mind omitting me from it? I don't ever want Reese Llewellyn to find us or have anything to hold over me."

"Ah, it will be a thrilling story, but made all the more so when I am the only hero."

Benedict chuckled as he watched the gondola disappear into the misty darkness of the early morning.

Nothing to Lose

"Now we have to get you out of here," said Emilio, motioning to the men who manned the oars.

Chapter 20

Sara had burst into tears when she'd heard the news on Monday that the charges against Ben would not be dropped. She was terrified by the prospect of him trying to escape from prison. So much could go wrong.

"Or, it could all go like clockwork and you and Ben will be headed to Portugal on Wednesday with a brilliant story to be able to tell your grandchildren," said Zina. "Stay hopeful Sara. Giving into despair will serve no one."

Zina was right and, once Sara had managed to pull herself together, she vowed to remain strong and positive until she was in Ben's arms again.

They received a message late in the day that Santi would arrive before daybreak on Tuesday and if all was clear he'd take Sara to the ship. He didn't want to leave it too long and run the risk of hitting obstacles. After all, it was a feast day and the streets would be teeming by afternoon. But he also didn't want to risk running into Llewellyn. So, Zina devised a system to alert Santi to Llewellyn's presence. It was simple, if the windows to the room Sara occupied were only half open, he was there. If they were fully open he was not.

Nothing to Lose

As luck would have it, Llewellyn hadn't visited Zina that evening.

Several hours before dawn, Zina had tapped on her door and entered.

"What are you doing up so early?" asked Sara.

"I could ask you the same thing of you, but I know the answer and I'm up for the same reason. I thought I'd sit with you and spend our last few hours together. You're the only other time traveler I've ever met and I liked having you here. I'll miss you."

"Oh, Zina, I'll miss you too. But you don't have to stay here. You should come with us."

Zina smiled. "I suppose I could, but I'm getting older. I only have a few years left to make what fortune I can as a courtesan."

"You know that the *Most Serene Republic of Venice* is in its decline."

"Yes, but like me, it has a few good years left."

"Still, you will always have a home with us, should you need it."

"And how will I find you?"

Sara smiled. "We'll settle near a port city, probably Baltimore or Philadelphia. I will send you a letter once we are there."

Zina frowned. "Just make certain nothing on it could identify you. As far as that goes, it is probably dangerous to use MacIan as a surname. It would make it easy for Llewellyn to track you down."

"I'm sure you're right, and Wells might not be safe either. I'm going to suggest we use my pseudonym."

"Your pseudonym? You said you were an author, but I assumed you were published under your own name. What is your pseudonym?"

"Arieta DeCosta."

"You aren't serious. You're Arieta DeCosta? I loved your books."

Sara laughed. "Well, I fear there won't be any more."

"But you should write more."

"I'm not sure my style of romance will be well received for the next couple hundred years or so."

"So, write them anyway. Lock them in a trunk and pass them down to your children. Then late in the twentieth century, one of your descendants can publish them."

Sara laughed. "I'll think about it. I suspect I may be a bit busy for the next few years."

Zina laughed too. "I hope so. I hope you have lots of children filling your home."

"So do I. But Zina, I'm serious. Come find us. Leave Venice before it falls to Napoleon."

"That's years away still. Plus, there's a war coming in America too. Maybe, in twenty-five years, after the Revolutionary War is over, I'll think about it. Venice will still be Venice until after that." Zina shrugged. "But, if I get bored with Venice before then, I may come earlier."

She and Zina chatted for several hours, making what had started as a painfully long night fly by.

Signore Santi arrived more than an hour before sunup.

"I'll go with you," said Zina. "I'm not ready to say goodbye."

Signore Santi shook his head. "I know you'd like to, but it poses too great a risk.

Tears filled Zina's eyes. "Then, my dear girl, give me a goodbye hug."

"I'm not saying goodbye, so I'll give you an 'until we meet again' hug."

When they'd said their farewells, Sara had climbed into the gondola with *Signore* Santi then the gondolier rowed away into the predawn quiet.

The gondolier took them to the Arsenale, where a longboat was moored and two sailors waited. *Signore* Santi helped her into the boat, retrieved a small chest from the gondola, and climbed in himself. It was still dark when they'd reached the merchant vessel moored in the lagoon and the longboat was hoisted up.

Signore Santi helped her onto the deck and, with the small chest under one arm, he introduced her to the captain, speaking English. "Sara, my dear, you have just boarded the Silky Selkie and the captain of this fine vessel is Edward MacLeod."

The captain gave a small bow. "Good morning, Miss Wells. 'Tis a pleasure to meet ye." He was a big man with thick sandy hair and a bushy reddish-gold beard, both shot with a fair bit of silver, and he spoke with a thick Scottish burr. "Ah sure, the Selkie *is* a fine vessel, but Santi could say nothing else for she was built by Santi and MacIan a few years ago. Welcome aboard."

"Thank you, sir. It's a pleasure to meet you too." She offered him her hand, and he took it, kissing the back.

"Now, lass, Santi has filled me in on the circumstances in which we find ourselves. So, for yer own safety, I'm going to show ye to yer cabin and I'll ask ye to stay there until we're under sail tomorrow."

"Certainly." Sara didn't look forward to spending the next twenty-four hours in a cramped ship's cabin, but she understood the necessity of it.

Emilio Santi said, "If you would wait just one moment, Captain. Sara, my dear, this chest is for Benedict from our partnership."

The captain took it from him. "I'll carry it down the passage for ye."

With his hands free, *Signore* Santi took both of hers in his and switched to Venetian. "I believe you and Benedict are soulmates, brought together and meant to stay together. I will miss him terribly, but he deserves this happiness. And now that I've come to know you, I will miss you too. I'll be staying on the ship tonight, to ensure Benedict is safely aboard tomorrow. But, as you will be hidden, I may not see you again. Go with God." He had kissed her on both cheeks.

"Thank you for everything you've done for us. I'm so sorry we have to leave like this."

"Don't think another moment about it. Look forward to the life ahead of you."

The captain showed her to the cabin she and Ben would share, and as promised, she hadn't left since then.

The cabin was bigger than she'd expected it to be. The captain had explained that it was the first mate's cabin, but he would kip in with the boatswain for this leg of the trip. Two chests of their belongings stood against one wall and a bed was built into the opposite wall. A small table and two chairs stood in the space between. A port hole by the bed let in light and fresh air.

Now nearly twenty-four hours had passed. If the escape had been successful, Ben should be here any minute. She knelt on the bed, looking out the porthole, hoping to see something. But it was dark and she wasn't even sure from which side of the ship they'd approach. Then the door opened behind her. In that instant, she prayed with everything in her that it was Benedict and not *Signore* Santi or the Captain.

~ *~

Sara spun around the instant he opened the door. "Oh, my beautiful girl. I have never been so happy to see someone in my life."

She threw herself into his arms and burst into tears. "Ben. Oh, Ben. I'm so sorry, this was all my fault."

He held her close. "No, Sara, don't cry. This was no one's fault. We decided together on the best course of action and I still think it was the right one. We gave Llewellyn a chance."

"I was so frightened that something would go wrong."

Immediately his mind went through the litany of things that nearly had gone wrong during the escape. But none of it mattered now. "I can only believe the universe is unfolding as it should."

"I suppose so, but I hope it unfolds with much less drama in the future."

He laughed. "As long as my future is with you, I don't care."

She stepped back so he could come all the way into the cabin and shut the door, then looked at him and frowned. "What are you wearing?"

He glanced down. "My best suit."

"You escaped from prison in your best suit?"

He laughed again. "No, I escaped from prison in the clothes I was wearing when last you saw me. But we changed into better clothes before we left the palace, so any passersby wouldn't realize we were prisoners."

"Well, let's get you out of them. You look exhausted."

"I'm not too exhausted to savor a few moments with the woman I love."

She smiled. "I haven't slept more than a few minutes at a time since last week. But all of a sudden, sleep is the last thing on my mind."

She stood on her tiptoes and kissed him as she began to divest him of his clothes.

He was only too happy to return the favor.

She became frustrated by the buttons on his breeches. "You know, there's a lot to be said for wearing less clothing. Kilts, for example. Dead sexy and much easier to remove."

He laughed. "Says the girl wearing layers of petticoats."

"By convention, not by choice."

Soon enough they were naked. She threaded her arms around his neck and kissed him, suckling on his lower lip. He ran his hands lightly up and down her back until she shivered with delight. Then he cupped his hands under her bottom and lifted her against his firm length.

Still locked in their embrace, he stepped toward the bed and lowered her onto it. "Oh, Sara, I want you so badly."

"Then take me."

"But, I want to cherish you, worship you."

"Ben, I want you too. I have craved your touch. Make love to me now. There will be plenty of time for gentle tenderness later."

At her urging, he entered her in one firm stroke. He made love to her without restraint and she responded in kind.

He groaned. "Sara, I can't hold back—"

"Then don't."

As he found his release, she reached between them, touching herself, reaching her own climax moments later.

They lay there panting as they drifted down from ecstasy.

He lifted his weight off of her and, lying on his side, pulled her against him. "Now, my precious girl, I would love to sleep with you in my arms for a few hours."

She snuggled against him and closed her eyes. "I don't have to be talked into that."

He planted a kiss behind her ear. "Besides, we'll need to rest up for tonight."

"Tonight?" she asked drowsily.

"Yes, I don't want to fall asleep in the middle of our wedding night."

"Our wedding night?"

He grinned. "Aye, once we're at sea the captain can marry us."

She smiled. "And he's willing to do it?"

"I'm sure he will be. We'll ask him to hear our vows this evening."

She yawned. "Good." She was asleep almost instantly.

But as tired as he was, Benedict didn't want to sleep just yet. He wanted to savor freedom and gaze at the woman he loved so dearly. He'd go to hell and back for her again, if he had to.

He heard the captain calling orders as the anchor was lifted, sails were hoisted, and they began to move. He knew this was his last chance to see Venice, so he carefully extricated himself from Sara's sleeping form, pulled on his clothes, and went up on the deck.

They were sailing out of the lagoon. He looked back towards Venice and to his surprise, felt nothing. He could see the Arsenale, where his shipyard was and where he had spent most of his days for the last fifteen years or so. He was proud of the business he'd help build and he would miss Emilio, but the sense of loss he'd expected to feel was absent. As they sailed past the Lido he again thought he'd feel a sense of loss. He loved it here. This had been his home. But his heart didn't ache as he thought it might. He saw the stretch of beach where Sara had taken him on a picnic and they had gone swimming. A grin spread across his face. If she were on that island, nothing would keep him from jumping overboard and swimming to her. That is when he realized Venice and its surroundings was not his home. His home was wherever Sara was, and she was asleep in the first mate's cabin. He turned away from the rail and descended the stairs without another glance backwards.

He undressed again and slipped back into bed beside her.

He was home.

~ * ~

They did sleep for several hours. They woke when the cabin boy knocked on the door near midday, bringing them bread, cheese, dried sausage, and a bottle of wine.

They ate, napped a little more, and then washed and dressed. Benedict suggested that they go up to deck for some air. They stood on the aft deck, looking backwards. The ship had sailed well into the Adriatic and Venice was far behind them, no longer visible.

After a few minutes, Sara looked up at him. "Will you miss it terribly?"

He smiled. "Honestly, no. I realized today that at some point in the last five and half weeks, you became the only thing that mattered to me. I love you and as long as we are together, home is where we make it."

A smile spread across her face and Benedict felt compelled to kiss her. But before he'd had his fill, Captain MacLeod came over to them and cleared his throat.

"Well now, I'd say ye both look as if ye had some much needed rest."

A warm blush spread across Sara's cheeks.

Benedict grinned. "Aye, we did, Captain."

"Good. And my cabin boy brought ye a bite to eat?"

"Aye, thank ye, sir," answered Sara.

"Good. Very good. Now, if the winds are in our favor, we should reach Lisbon in two or three weeks. We have some cargo to deliver there. Then I suspect, I could take on enough goods there to make a trip to the colonies worth my while."

"Really?" Asked Benedict. "That would be brilliant."

"Aye. I think it's the best plan. Santi told me about Llewellyn. I've never sought to do business with him because of his reputation for having a vile temper. But when I heard he wouldn't let ye marry this wee lass simply because ye're a Scot, well that's beyond the pale. I won't ever do business with him. However, having said that, there are quite a few merchant vessels that often sail in and out of Lisbon whose captains do."

"I knew we might run into that in any major port. I'd decided we would have to bide our time until the right ship came along."

"Still, there isn't a man on this ship who would ever utter a word about ye. But even if you met a captain who wouldn't ever reveal where you'd gone to Llewellyn, there is no guarantee that his men would be equally circumspect if the payoff was sufficiently large. Then there is the chance that a captain or crew from a merchant ship in port at Lisbon might recognize ye and pass the word on to him. Nay, the risk is too great. So, we'll make certain ye aren't seen in Lisbon and head straight to the new world after that."

Benedict offered the man his hand. "Thank you, Captain. I'm in your debt."

"Nay, lad, just be sure to give me a good deal on a new ship if the Selkie ever becomes unseaworthy."

Benedict grinned. "It's a deal. Now I must ask for one last favor."

"Ye want to marry the wee lassie clinging to yer arm?"

Benedict laughed. "Yes, sir. If it isn't too much trouble."

"No trouble at all. How about we gather on the bow just before sunset, then ye can join me for a wedding supper before retiring."

He glanced down at Sara who nodded and gifted him with a brilliant smile. "That will be perfect, sir."

And so it was that several hours later, they stood on the bow of the ship, in front of the captain and his officers, and exchanged their wedding vows as the setting sun lit the western horizon with shades of pink and orange.

"Benedict MacIan, will ye have this woman to be thy wedded wife, will ye love her, and honor her, keep her and guard her, in health and in sickness, as a husband should a wife, and forsaking all others on account of her, keep ye only unto her, so long as ye both shall live."

"I will."

"And Sara Wells, will ye have this man to thy wedded husband, will ye obey him, and serve him, love, honor, and keep him in sickness and in health; and, forsaking all other on account of him, keep ye only unto him, so long as ye both shall live?"

"I will."

The captain reached into the pocket of his waistcoat and pulled out a pair of gold rings. "*Signore* Santi gave these to me. He said he suspected ye'd be needing them. If I were a priest, I might have some prayer at the ready to bless these rings, but I'd surely give the good Lord a chuckle if I tried. Still, I figure there's a fair bit of love in them. *Signore* Santi knew ye loved each other and would want them as a symbol of that love. Then too, he loved ye both and wanted ye to have them. It was his way of sending ye off with love. When ye look at them remember that. But also remember that a ring is a circle, with no start and no end. And that is the true nature of love. It keeps going with no start and no end. Love each other as you have been loved. Love yer children should the Lord so bless ye. Love yer neighbors. And here's the hardest bit, love yer enemies. I can't say that I've mastered that one, but it's what we're called to do. And with that, Benedict, take this ring and place it on the third finger of Sara's left hand and repeat after me."

Benedict did as he asked, repeating the words, "Sara Wells, with this ring, I thee wed, in the name of the Father and the Son and the Holy Spirit." He slipped the ring on her finger.

Then Sara took the larger gold ring and repeated the words, "Benedict MacIan, with this ring, I thee wed, in the name of the Father and the Son and the Holy Spirit."

The old captain beamed at them. "Benedict and Sara, you are now husband and wife. Kiss yer bride, lad."

Cradling her head with one hand, Benedict leaned down and kissed his lovely wife as the sun dipped below the horizon.

~ * ~

Sara couldn't imagine a more romantic wedding and she had married quite a few couples in her books. But this was her wedding to the man she cherished. Countless miracles had occurred to bring them to this moment. When he gave her that first kiss as husband and wife, as the sun set and the stars began to twinkle, the magic was complete.

Dinner with the captain and his officers was delicious and much to her delight, didn't drag on. Not long after they had finished with dessert, the captain offered one more toast and bid them goodnight.

In no time, she was alone again with her beloved. "Now, my darling husband, you can take all the time you need to worship me."

He gave a low chuckle before doing just that. He took her higher and higher, never quite letting her go. Hovering on the edge was heaven but eventually, she could stand it no more. "Benedict, please...

"Anything you wish, my beloved." He entered her with long firm strokes, finally allowing her to topple over the edge of bliss.

As she lay in his arms savoring the afterglow, he kissed her temple and whispered, "I love you."

She turned her head to him and planted a soft kiss on his lips. "I love you, too." She sighed and settled into his embrace.

Soon his breathing became slow and steady as he drifted to sleep, but sleep didn't come quite as swiftly for her. She listened to the sound of the waves hitting the hull and took a deep breath in, savoring the ocean air. She smiled to herself. When she had flown to Venice, this was not the cruise she had expected. But a wise old woman with a pocket watch had different plans for her. *Thank you, Gertrude.* Then she drifted off to sleep, lulled by the gentle motion of the ship.

Epilogue

The DeCosta Farm, Mount Holly, NJ
August 1788

The cock crowed, rousing Sara from sleep as the sun was rising. She lay quietly next to Ben for a moment, remembering the dream she'd been having. It was an odd dream. She was in the twenty-first century, in her apartment outside of Baltimore.

Over the years, she'd had lots of dreams about her own time. In the early years, when they lived in Philadelphia where Ben worked as a shipbuilder, they were nightmares. She had somehow uttered the return word and was yanked back to her old life, into her old body. She searched desperately for Ben, but couldn't find him. He was lost to her. She'd wake from these dreams, terrified and in a panic, only to find herself safe within the circle of his arms.

After a few years they went away, but returned with vigor twelve years later as life under British rule became more untenable. Even though they had changed their surname to DeCosta when they arrived in the colonies, Sara lived with fear that Llewellyn might somehow find them. Finally, they decided to leave Philadelphia. Benedict took on a partner and put the management of his shipyard into his capable hands. They bought a farm thirty miles away, in New Jersey, near the village of Mount Holly. Even though they were still under British rule in New Jersey, things were not as tense out in the country as they had been in Philadelphia.

They weren't terribly far from the Delaware River and from there he could sail down to Philadelphia fairly quickly, but he only did this one day a week or even less as time passed. Benedict was forty-four now and instead of spending his days building ships, he created a thriving business making beautiful furniture.

After that, the dreams changed. They were no longer nightmares. She would find herself in the house she grew up in. Her parents and brother were still alive. They hadn't changed but she had. She was in Ceres Llewellyn's body and yet that didn't seem to matter. They knew who she was. Sometimes Ben would be with her in these dreams. And as time passed, her children would be there too, to the delight of their grandparents and uncle. These had been very good dreams, but she hadn't had one in years. Maybe that was because she was a grandmother herself now.

She and Ben had six children. Their oldest, Lily, was twenty-eight and married to Daniel, a farmer whose land bordered theirs. She and Daniel had three children ranging from a year old to six.

Joshua was twenty-six. He had been named for her brother and as he grew, she was amazed at how much like his uncle he became. Joshua too was married to his beloved Beth and they had one three-year-old girl and a child on the way. He worked in the family business with Ben.

Their third child, Emil, was twenty-four now. He had gone to university and had become a lawyer. He was working for a lawyer in Burlington, less than ten miles away. He wasn't married yet, but was courting the lawyer's daughter.

Rosina, their fourth child was twenty-two and had just married the town blacksmith's son in June.

Their two youngest children, twin boys named Ian and James, were nineteen and had given Sara more gray hair than all the rest of them. Both boys were working as apprentices to Ben and Joshua now.

Ben interrupted her musings. "What's the matter?"

She smiled, rose up on an elbow, and gave him a kiss. "Nothing. Why?"

"You normally get right up. It seemed like something was on your mind."

"I was just thinking about a dream I was having."

"About what?"

"My old life."

"It's been a long time since you've had one of those."

"I know. And this one wasn't like any of the others."

"What was different?"

"It was in the future. What I mean is…well it seemed like it was *after* my trip to Venice, as if I hadn't accepted the pocket watch. I've often thought about that moment. About what would have happened if I had turned down the offer. One single choice changed the entire course of my life."

"Well, thank God you made the right choice, because I can't imagine ever living without you." He kissed her.

"I can't either. And but for the grace of God, I might have lost you in those first few days."

Benedict grinned. "The grace of God and the audacity of Giacomo Casanova."

"The things you've told me about him are so contrary to the kind of man I'd always thought he was. I know I've said it before, but I would like to have met him."

"And I know I've said it before, but I'm glad you didn't. The charming bastard might have stolen you away from me."

"Not a chance." She kissed him.

"Ah, now that's not the kind of kiss that will convince me of that."

"Oh, it isn't is it? Then how about this one." She put a hand on his cheek and gave him a scorching kiss.

"That was much better."

She smiled. "What were we talking about?"

"I think it was about how I'm going to make love to my wife as the sun rises."

"That's a very good idea."

A Note from the Author

I hope you enjoyed this trip to the past with the pocket watch.

I wanted to share a few tidbits about the historical details of this story, particularly where Giacomo Casanova is concerned.

When I was trying to figure out how to break Benedict out of jail, I read a book called *The Story of My Escape: from the Prisons of the Republic of Venice otherwise known as "The Leads,"* written by Casanova in 1788, and translated by Andrew Lawston. It starts with Casanova's arrest and details both his imprisonment and escape, from his point of view. The book was extremely detailed and occasionally very funny. But the most surprising thing to me was how completely likable Casanova was. If you are interested in learning more about him, I highly recommend reading *The Story of My Escape*.

As I read the book, I realized that Casanova's escape was so incredibly improbable it couldn't happen twice. So, the way forward seemed obvious—Benedict needed to escape with him. This is where I took a bit of literary license.

Casanova was arrested by the Venetian Republic and charged with *an affront to religion and common decency.* He was found guilty, sentenced to five years imprisonment in *The Leads.* And as unbelievable as the escape I described sounded, it really did happen and I changed very few of the details. The major departure from the real event is when it actually occurred. This portion of The Choice takes place in July and August of 1758. Casanova was arrested on July 26, 1755, and the escape started on October 31, 1756. He walked out of the Doge's Palace early in the morning on All Saints Day, November 1. So, I adjusted the dates a little.

Now back to the book. If you declined the pocket watch first and have already read what happens to Sara if she stays in her time, then you know both stories now. I encourage you to click here if you want to read more about me or you'd like to see what other books Duncurra offers.

If you would like to find out what would have happened if Sara had declined the pocket watch, you may enjoy reading *What if I Fall in Love.*

About The Author

Ceci started her career as an oncology nurse at a leading research hospital, and eventually became a successful medical writer. In 1991, she married a young Irish carpenter whom she met when his brother married her dear friend. They raised their family in central New Jersey but now live with their dogs and birds in paradise, also known as southwest Florida. Although still working occasionally as a consultant in the pharmaceutical industry, Ceci spends most of her time now writing "happily ever afters."

Her bestselling Duncurra series, _Highland Solution, Highland Courage,_ and _Highland Intrigue_ are available as e-books, audiobooks, and paperbacks. There are also inspirational versions of each of these which close the bedroom door (_Highland Solution – Inspirational, Highland Courage – Inspirational_, and _Highland Intrigue – Inspirational_). Ceci will be revisiting the Duncurra world in the Duncurra Legacy series. The first novel, _Tomas – A Highland Redemption,_ will be released in the summer of 2017.

The Fated Hearts series begins with Ceci's novella _Highland Revenge_ (originally appearing in _Highland Winds, The Scrolls of Cridhe_ – Volume 1) and continues with _Highland Echoes_ and _Highland Angels_.

If you enjoyed _The Choice_, look for the other Pocket

Watch Chronicles. *The Pocket Watch* and *The Midwife* are available on Amazon as e-books, paperbacks, and audiobooks. *The Christmas Present* is available as an e-book. *Once Found* is available as an e-book and a paperback. The audio version of ***Once Found*** is available for FREE here, on Duncurra's YouTube channel.

Don't miss the Duncurra YouTube channel

- https://www.youtube.com/duncurra!

You'll find videos of Scotland, Scottish words of the day explained, free audiobooks, and much more

Follow Ceci at:

Website: www.cecigiltenan.com
Facebook: https://www.facebook.com/cgiltenan
Twitter: https://twitter.com/CeciGiltenan

If you enjoyed *Nothing to Lose*, you might be curious about what would have happened if Sara had accepted the watch and travelled back in time. To find out, read *What if I Fall*.

You also might enjoy reading the other Pocket Watch Chronicles:

If you enjoyed The Choice, you might like to read the other
Pocket Watch Chronicles

The Pocket Watch

When Maggie Mitchell is transported to the thirteenth century
Highlands, will Laird Logan Carr help mend her broken heart or
put it in more danger than before?

Generous, kind, and loving, Maggie nearly always puts the needs
of others first. So when a mysterious elderly woman gives her an
extraordinary pocket watch, telling her it's a conduit to the past,
Maggie agrees to give the watch a try, if only to disprove the
woman's delusion.

But it works.

Maggie finds herself in the thirteenth-century Scottish Highlands
with a handsome warrior who clearly despises her. Her tender soul
is caught between her own desire and the disaster she could cause
for others. Will she find a way to resolve the trouble and return
home within the allotted sixty days? Or will someone worthy earn
her heart forever?

The Midwife

Can a twenty-first century independent woman find her true destiny in thirteenth-century Scotland?

At his father's bidding, Cade MacKenzie begs a favor from Laird Macrae—Lady MacKenzie desperately needs the renowned Macrae midwife. Laird Macrae has no intention of sending his clan's best, instead he passes off Elsie, a young woman with little experience, as the midwife they seek.

But fate—in the form of a mysterious older woman and an extraordinary pocket watch—steps in.

Elizabeth Quinn, a disillusioned obstetrician, is transported to the thirteenth century. She switched souls with Elsie as the old woman said she would, but other things don't go quite as expected. Perhaps most unexpected was falling in love.

Once Found

Elsie thought she had found love.

The handsome young minstrel awoke her desire and his music fed her soul. But just as love was blossoming, the inconceivable happened—Elsie awoke more than seven hundred years in the future, in the body of Dr. Elizabeth Quinn.

Gabriel Soldani thought he had found love several times, only to have it slip from his grasp. In medical school, he had fallen hard for Elizabeth Quinn, but their careers led them in different directions. When their paths cross again, he hopes they've been given another chance.

There's only one problem…the woman he's never forgotten doesn't remember him.

Once love is found…and then lost…can it be found again?

The Christmas Present

A Pocket Watch Novella

Faced with an empty nest, and heartbroken, Anita Lewis is given the chance to experience Christmas in another time with the help of a mysterious old woman and a pocket watch.

The gift she receives is priceless as she rediscovers the magic of Christmas in the past.

.

Other Books by Ceci Giltenan

The Duncurra Series

Highland Solution

Laird Niall MacIan needs Lady Katherine Ruthven's dowry to relieve his clan's crushing debt, but he has no intention of giving her his heart in the bargain.

Niall MacIan, a Highland laird, desperately needs funds to save his impoverished clan. Lady Katherine Ruthven, a lowland heiress, is rumored to be "unmarriageable" and her uncle hopes to be granted her title and lands when the king sends her to a convent. King David II, anxious to strengthen his alliances, sees a solution that will give Ruthven the title he wants, and MacIan the money he needs. Laird MacIan will receive Lady Katherine's hand along with her substantial dowry and her uncle will receive her lands and title.

Lady Katherine must forfeit everything in exchange for a husband who does not want to be married and believes all women to be self-centered and deceitful. Can the lovely and gentle Katherine mend his heart and build a life with him or will he allow the treachery of others to destroy them?

The first book in the Duncurra Series, available as e-book, audiobook and paperback. An Inspirational Version is also available which has been edited to remove explicit intimate scenes.

Highland Courage

Her parents want a betrothal, but Mairead MacKenzie can't get married without revealing her secret and no man will wed her once he knows.

Plain in comparison to her siblings and extremely reserved, Mairead has been called "MacKenzie's Mouse" since she was a child. No one knows the reason for her timidity and she would just as soon keep it that way. When her parents arrange a betrothal to Laird Tadhg Matheson, she is horrified. She only sees one way to prevent an old secret from becoming a new scandal.

Tadhg Matheson admires and respects the MacKenzies. While an alliance with them through marriage to Mairead would be in his clan's best interest, he knows Laird MacKenzie seeks a closer alliance with another clan. When Tadhg learns of her terrible shyness and her youngest brother's fears about her, Tadhg offers for her anyway.

Secrets always have a way of revealing themselves. With Tadhg's unconditional love, can Mairead find the strength and courage she needs to handle the consequences when they do?

Available as e-book, audiobook and paperback.

Highland Intrigue

Lady Gillian MacLennan's clan needs a leader, but the last person on earth she wants as their laird is Fingal MacIan. She can neither forgive nor forget that his mother killed her father, and, by doing so, created Clan MacLennan's current desperate circumstances.

King David knows a weak clan, without a laird, can change quickly from a simple annoyance to a dangerous liability, and he cannot ignore the turmoil. The MacIan's owe him a great debt, so when he makes Fingal MacIan laird of clan MacLennan and requires that he marry Lady Gillian, Fingal is in no position to refuse.

In spite of the challenge, Fingal is confident he can rebuild her clan, ease her heartache, and win her affection. However, just as love awakens, the power struggle takes a deadly turn. Can he protect her from the unknown long enough to uncover the plot against them? Or will all be lost, destroying the happiness they seek in each other's arms?

Available as e-book, audiobook and paperback

Duncurra Legacy Novels

Highland Redemption

Tomas's life changed forever when at the age of seven he was adopted by Laird and Lady MacIan ending the abuse he'd suffered at Ambrose Ruthven's hand. He'd never looked back and never intended to

But fate had other plans...

Now, nineteen years later, he runs headlong into his past. The Ruthvens are in trouble and Tomas is in a position to help them. But can he set aside his hatred for Laird Ruthven for the good of the clan into which he was born?

Fate always adds a twist...

Laird Ruthven's daughter is not what Tomas expected. Vida Ruthven is sweet, smart, and utterly irresistible.

Now, Tomas must choose between being the savior or taking the ultimate revenge.

The Fated Hearts Series

Highland Revenge

Does he hate her clan enough to visit his vengeance on her? Or will he listen to her secret and his own heart's yearning?

Hatred lives and breathes between medieval clans who often don't remember why feuds began in the shadowed past.

But Eoin MacKay remembers.

He will never forget how he was treated by Bhaltair MacNicol—

the acting head of Clan MacNicol. He was lucky to escape alive, and vows to have revenge.

Years later, as laird of Clan MacKay, he gets his chance when he captures Lady Fiona MacNicol. His desire for revenge is strong but he is beguiled by his captive.

Can he forget his stubborn hatred long enough to listen to the secret she has kept for so long? And once he knows the truth, can he show her she is not alone and forsaken? In the end, is he strong enough to fight the combined hostilities and age-old grudges that demand he give her up?

Highland Revenge is available as an e-book, audio book and paperback.

Highland Echoes

Love echoes.

Grace Breive is strong and independent because she has to be. She has a wee daughter to care for and, having lost her parents and husband, has no one else on whom she can rely. Driven from the only home she has ever known, she travels to Castle Sutherland to find a grandmother she never knew she had.

As Laird Sutherland's heir, Bram Sutherland understands his obligation to enter into a political marriage for the good of the clan, but he is captivated by the beautiful and resilient young mother.

Will Bram and Grace follow the dictates of their hearts, or will echoes from the past force them apart?

Highland Echoes is available as an e-book, audio book and paperback.

Highland Angels

Anna MacKay fears the MacLeods. Andrew MacLeod fears love.

Anna, angry with her brother, took a walk to cool her temper. She had no intention of venturing so close to MacLeod territory—until she saw a wee lad fall through the ice.

Andrew becomes enraged when it appears the MacKay lass has abducted his son, his last precious connection to the wife he lost—until he learns the truth. Anna risked her life to save his beloved child.

Now there is a chance to end the generations old hate and fear between their clans.

Fate connects them. The desire for peace binds them. Will a rival tear them apart?

Highland Angels is available as an e-book, audio book and paperback.

About Duncurra

Duncurra is a small independent publishing company. We highly value the heart and soul, energy, time, and talent that our authors pour into their stories. Unlike many independent publishers, we help authors build their readership by investing significantly in marketing platforms to complement the author's own promotional efforts.

We are particularly proud of our YouTube presence and ever increasing subscribership there, which is unique to the publishing industry.

Whether you are a reader, an established author, or an aspiring author, we have a lot to offer. We take the reader experience to a new level, connecting authors and readers in unprecedented ways.

Visit our website at www.duncurra.com.

To stay up to date on all Duncurra releases, sales, giveaways, and more. Sign up for our newsletter here:
https://tinyletter.com/duncurra

Experience the difference.

Experience Duncurra!

Other titles published by Duncurra LLC

Award Winning, New York Times Bestselling Author

Kathryn Lynn Davis

Highland Awakening

Can the transforming power of magic help two people on a perilous journey create a miracle—even when one of them doesn't believe?

Since she lost her brother and nearly her father, Esmé Rose fears the world beyond her family and her garden. But one year when winter clings overlong, a dream begins to haunt her, forcing her to take a journey and face a challenge more difficult than she could ever imagine.

Magnus MacLeod is a skilled healer, always curious to know more. He, too, is called by a dream he doesn't quite believe in, despite its physical effects on him. He and Esmé travel a treacherous road that takes them to a magical place. There they must put aside their feelings for one another—and their difference in beliefs—long enough to make a miracle.

Sing to Me of Dreams

One woman's journey of discovery...through all the mysteries of the human heart.

As a child, Saylah held the magic and wisdom of her Salish Indian people. But when tragedy ravages the Salish, she must leave them for the world of the Ivys – an English/Scottish family whose traditions are as strange to her as her spirit world is to them. The Ivys have come to fertile British Columbia in search of paradise, but the secrets and mysteries surrounding them are overwhelming – until Saylah comes to help them understand the darkness holding them back.

Frustrated Julian Ivy, in whom sophistication and fury entwine, is drawn to Saylah's healing strength and disquieting beauty. Through sorrow and elation, the two discover the fullness of love...but no one can resolve for her the contradictions of her birthright. Following the songs of her heritage, she will finally make the most wrenching choice of all...

Weave for Me a Dream

The long awaited sequel to Sing to Me of Dreams!

Saylah's journey continues as secrets woven in the past threaten the fabric of her family.

Victoria, Vancouver Island, B.C.

1895

Saylah Ivy, once shaman of her Salish tribe, now wife and mother, continues her journey of discovery, following her white husband

Julian as he seeks new adventure in the city.

Where Saylah and their daughter Illiann must meet the challenge of living two lives: both Salish and White, while facing prejudice, discovery and danger along the way. Julian and their son Kit confront a powerful enemy who threatens their very lives. Meanwhile, secrets from their pasts haunt them daily.

The family must protect themselves from threats to both their bodies and their souls. They must battle their enemies to stay true to who they have become, and to discover a place where their hearts are at peace. Perhaps hardest of all, they must find a way to forgive those who hurt them long ago.

Award Winning, Bestselling Author

Lily Baldwin

Highland Outlaw Series

(All of the Highland Outlaw series are complete standalone stories and can be read in any order.)

Jack: A Scottish Outlaw

Freedom is not won…it is stolen

Jack MacVie and his brother are thieves, robbing English nobles on the road north into Scotland. They're about to attack the Redesdale carriage when another band of villains, after more than

Lady Redesdale's coin, sweeps down and steals their prize. Despite his hatred for the English, Jack's conscience forces him to kidnap the lady to save her life.

In the aftermath of the Berwick massacre, Lady Isabella Redesdale's world is shattered. Her mother is dead, her father lost to grief, and she's risking it all, journeying north into war-torn Scotland to be with her sister.

Although they come from different worlds, Jack and Isabella are more alike than they first realize. They both crave freedom from war and despair, but in a world where kings reign and birth dictates one's station, freedom is not won, it is stolen.

Quinn: A Scottish Outlaw

He is an outlaw…And the only man she can trust.

Quinn MacVie is in pursuit of a prize, but it is unlike any plunder he has stolen before. He seeks neither gold nor jewels, but something infinitely more valuable—Lady Catarina Ravensworth. Sent by the lady's sister, who fears Catarina is in danger, Quinn's mission is to steal the lady away from Ravensworth castle. But nothing there is as Quinn expected.

Lady Catarina has been accused of a horrific crime and is forced to run or face a fate worse than death.

But she is not alone.

Thief and Scottish rebel, Quinn MacVie, is at her side. With a price on her head, they must disappear into the wilds of the Scottish Highlands where the only thing greater than the danger following at their heels is the desire burning in their hearts.

Rory: A Scottish Outlaw

Lady Alexandria MacKenzie is one of Abbot Matthew's network of rebels, fighting for Scottish independence. When her father dies, leaving their clan without a laird, she asks the abbot for aid in finding a husband. He sends her a selection of three noblemen from which to choose. Accompanying them is secret agent and reputed rake, Rory MacVie, who must assist Alexandria with a perilous mission for Scotland. But the abbot makes one point very clear--Rory is not a potential suitor.

This is a passionate story of honor, rebellion, and forbidden love.

Alec: A Scottish Outlaw

Two broken hearts unite, becoming one love that will last forever.

Sold from one ruthless master to another, Joanie is a servant who has lived her whole life in fear. When Randolph Tweed, an English merchant with cold, unfeeling eyes, buys her, she fears she has fallen into the hands of her cruelest master yet. But what she doesn't realize is that Randolph is actually Alec MacVie, Scottish spy and rebel.

The first time Alec sees Joanie is in his dreams. He has a vision of a young woman standing on a bridge alone, bleeding, and broken hearted. He must rescue her, and when he does he soon realizes she holds the power to rescue him right back.

Join Alec and Joanie on a journey of healing, passion, and hope, where their love and strength forge a new destiny for themselves and for Scotland.

Stephanie Joyce Cole

Compass North

Can you ever run away from your own life?

Reeling from the shock of a suddenly shattered marriage, Meredith flees as far from her home in Florida as she can get without a passport: to Alaska.

After a freak accident leaves her presumed dead, she stumbles into a new identity and a new life in a quirky small town. Her friendship with a fiery and temperamental artist and her growing worry for her elderly, cranky landlady pull at the fabric of her carefully guarded secret. When a romance with a local fisherman unexpectedly blossoms, Meredith struggles to find a way to meld her past and present so that she can move into the future she craves. But someone is looking for her, someone who will threaten Meredith's dream of a reinvented life.

James Donbar

Pacificus

What happens when a group of the world's wealthiest people desire a haven for themselves and their assets?

Pacificus is built one hundred miles off the coast of Ecuador. This manmade island is governed solely by a set of principles and relies on the common sense of its inhabitants instead of laws.

What could go wrong?

For Gaspar Delgado, the island's administrator, nothing. He need only find the balance between the privileged indulgence of its residents and order.

However, Conrad Silverstein, a smug self-serving newspaper editor, is certain something sinister lurks under the high-minded values supposedly espoused by Pacificans and sends reporter, Alicia Jones, to find out what it is.

Will this utopia be threatened by those willing to exploit liberty at any expense?

Ford Murphy

<u>Taking the Town</u>

Lissadown, Ireland 1986.

A ruthless, violent criminal gang has held the small midlands town in its grip for too long.

Innocents have been maimed, raped, killed.

Law enforcement is paralyzed.

Finn Lane has had enough. A newcomer to Lissadown and an expert MMA fighter, Finn can't be intimidated. Keeping his head down and minding his own business is not an option. The gang may think they own the town and everyone in it but those days are coming to an end.

He will have vengeance…

MJ Platt

Somewhere Montana

Can Callum "Mac" Maclain make Sage Burnett believe in his love for her and
save her from her stalker?

Escaping from a stalker, Sage Burnett crashes her plane on a mountain, part of the ranch owned by the man who rejected her eight years ago. She still loves him and prays he isn't around because she dreads facing him to only have him reject her again.

Callum "Mac" MacLain, the ranch owner, a Marine home on medical leave rescues her from the mountain. He persuades her to stay until she heals. He realizes he is still in love with her. Can he save her from her stalker and convince her his love is real?

B.J. Scott

Talisman of Light

Will changing the Past destroy their future?

Intent on setting a wrong to right, Alex Innes flies to Scotland to return an Ancient Talisman to its rightful resting place. But his plane crashes and he finds himself in twelfth century Scotland, where winter holds the country in its icy grip and only one maiden can set it free. Ciara Dunmore offers her life to appease the winter hag on the Imbolc Festival, but Alex has different plans for the beguiling lass who has captured his heart. Will changing the past destroy their future?

Forever and Beyond

Katherine MacDonald trades her luxury Manhattan apartment, high paying job, and abusive fiancé for what she believes is a rundown estate, deep in the Scottish Highlands, unaware that her future, and perhaps her very life, depends on secrets deeply rooted in the past.

When she discovers a ring with a sentimental inscription and a journal written by one of her ancestors within the ancient croft, she suddenly finds herself in fourteenth century Scotland where she comes face to face with Ayden MacAndrews, a braw Highlander who has haunted her dreams since she was a child.

Will Katherine and Ayden be able to right an ancient wrong? Will their love stand the test of time?

Jennifer Siddoway

Dealing with the Devil

Wynnona Hendricks has some shocking surprises in store. Struggling to figure out her comatose mother's secret, Wynn gets more than she bargained for, and ends up caught between the realms of Heaven, Hell, and Earth, fighting for her life.

Family and friends are stunned by her bizarre behavior; the only one who believes in her is Caleb, an angel who chose to spare her life. But by saving her, he may have started a war between the factions, throwing the Mortal Realm into mayhem. Wynn discovers new allies, new enemies—including her own human weakness—and new powers as she fights to protect her family from being ripped apart.

Coming in June, part two of the Earthwalker Trilogy: The Devil's Due

www.ingramcontent.com/pod-product-compliance
Lightning Source LLC
Chambersburg PA
CBHW031658170626
46808CB00005B/1502